CANDIDE

CANDIDE

VOLTAIRE

This edition published in 2022 by Arcturus Publishing Limited
26/27 Bickels Yard, 151–153 Bermondsey Street,
London SE1 3HA

Typesetting by Palimpsest Book Production Limited

Cover design: Peter Ridley
Cover illustration: Peter Gray
Design: Beatriz Custodio

AD005950UK

Printed in the UK

MIX
Paper from
responsible sources
FSC® C018072
www.fsc.org

CONTENTS

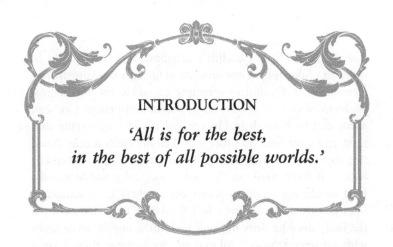

INTRODUCTION

'All is for the best, in the best of all possible worlds.'

Voltaire's *Candide* is one of the best-known and most influential narratives of the eighteenth century. The young Candide, thrown out of his adopted home after a sexual indiscretion with the baron's daughter, ranges over much of the world trying to win her back. He is carried along on a torrent of action, improbable in the extreme and packed almost beyond endurance with atrocities and barbarity. Yet *Candide* is not a novel in the modern sense of the word. The central characters of the young Candide, his beloved Cunégonde, his tutor Pangloss and his companions Martin and the old woman are not fully drawn personalities and their exploits are barely credible. Instead, it is a *conte philosophique* – a philosophical tale – that uses narrative to make a point and prompt deep thinking. The tale satirizes a popular philosophical position which Voltaire had himself once espoused, and calls on us to negotiate metaphysical issues that affect everyone. The universal relevance of the questions addressed in Candide has ensured the tale's enduring appeal for 250 years.

Candide, or Optimism

The subtitle of *Candide*, 'Optimism', defines the outlook of the young hero and refers to the eighteenth-century doctrine of Optimism, put forward by Gottfried Leibniz in his book

Theodicy in 1710. Candide's attempts to root his life in optimist philosophy come unstuck as he faces one catastrophe after another. Optimism attempts to tackle the theological problem of evil – how an all-powerful and benign God can allow evil to flourish in His created world – by saying that there can have been no other way. Leibniz spells it out: 'Now, this supreme wisdom [God] ... cannot but have chosen the best ... if there were not the best among all possible worlds, God would not have produced any ... there is an infinitude of possible worlds, among which God must needs have chosen the best, since he does nothing without acting in accordance with supreme reason.'[1] All evil and misfortune, then, have a purpose and are necessary even though we may not be able to discern their purpose.

Early in his life, Voltaire was swayed by Leibniz's argument, but experience eroded his confidence in the optimist philosophy. He found it untenable in the face of the trauma and suffering that fills human life. For Voltaire, the final death knell for optimism was sounded by the terrible earthquake that struck Lisbon in Portugal on 1 November 1755. Up to 60,000 people died in the earthquake itself, in the ensuing tsunami and in the fires which razed the ruins of the city. Sir Thomas Kendrick wrote at the time that the earthquake 'shocked western civilization more than any other event since the fall of Rome in the fifth century'. In a letter to a friend in December 1755, Voltaire wrote, 'Optimism and all-is-well got it in the neck,' and in his poem on the earthquake, he pondered:

Why do we suffer under a just Lord?
This is the knot which must be untied.

---

1   G. W. Leibniz, *Theodicy: Essays on the Justice of God and the Freedom of Man in the Origin of Evil*, translated C. J. Gerhardt, Routledge and Kegan Paul, London, 1952, p.128.

It was the knot which would lie at the heart of *Candide*, published in 1759.

Committed optimists explained away even a calamity of this magnitude. Jean-Jacques Rousseau, philosopher and author of *The Social Contract*, argued that God was not concerned with the fate of individuals. He said it was the fault of the inhabitants of Lisbon for building homes that were not earthquake-proof and for crowding into the city instead of living naturally in the countryside. The optimist view of the catastrophe is parodied in *Candide* (p.28): 'all this is for the best, for if there is a volcano in Lisbon, then it cannot be anywhere else; it is impossible that things should not be as they are, for all is well.'

Dr Pangloss teaches Candide that 'there is no effect without a cause ... in this best of all possible worlds' (p.14). Candide initially accepts Dr Pangloss's optimist view without question, but increasingly he struggles to accommodate the hardships and cruelties he witnesses and endures. Like the Roman Emperor Diocletian, who ruled for twenty-one years and then retired to grow cabbages, at the very end of his adventures Candide retires to tend his garden. He is resigned to the failure of the doctrine of optimism and has found that humankind endures, rather than triumphs over, adversity. This endurance is a necessity: it does not spring from any great philosophical idea, but it is all that is possible.

Voltaire begins undermining the optimist view from the first chapter. To the familiar trope accepted and propounded by Candide, 'the best of all possible worlds', he adds the ridiculous extension 'the Baron's castle was the most magnificent of castles, and his Lady the best of all possible baronesses.' (p.14). He gives Pangloss a ludicrous justification of Leibniz's assertion that everything has a purpose and there is 'sufficient reason' for the world being as it is:

'It is proven', he said, 'that things cannot be otherwise than as they are; for all being created for an end, all is

necessarily for the best end. Observe, that noses have been formed to carry spectacles, so we have spectacles. Legs are visibly designed for breeches and we wear breeches.' (p.14)

Candide's adventures

The extremes of suffering to which Candide is exposed would be more than enough to disillusion most optimists. Already, by the end of the second chapter, he has lost his beloved, been exiled, been press-ganged into the army and run the gauntlet of 2,000 men (twice), receiving 4,000 blows 'which laid bare all his muscles and nerves, from the nape of his neck right down to his rump' (p.18). The ensuing narrative continues the catalogue of disasters, tragedies and agonies visited on Candide, his companions and his beloved, Cunégonde. All these are told in rollicking, speedy succession. The tale owes much to the picaresque style epitomized in English in the novels of Smollett and Defoe, in which episode is piled upon episode in an implausible, unending stream. There is little time for development of character or evocation of scene and sentiment.

Who was Voltaire?

François-Marie Arouet, born either 21 November or 20 February 1694, was the son either of the notary François-Marie Arouet or of an officer called Rochebrune – thus Voltaire was of uncertain birth date, uncertain parentage and was not called Voltaire. His mother died when he was seven, and he did not get on with his legal father. Instead he formed a close attachment to his godfather, the epicurean Abbé de Châteauneuf, who introduced him to the famous courtesan and literary figure Ninon de Lenclos (she was 84 at the time). In her will, Ninon left the young Voltaire money to buy books. He attended the Jesuit college in Paris, where he enthusiastically embraced the culture and society but

rejected the religious aspects of his education. He was permanently affected by the last years of the reign of Louis XIV and the religious persecution that he witnessed. He spoke out for civil liberties of all types, and against religious persecution, throughout his life.

The young Arouet took a job as an ambassadorial secretary in the Netherlands, but the scandal of his infatuation with a young woman had him sent back to Paris. There he made a name for himself writing witty epigrams, but was soon in trouble for mocking the regent, the Duc d'Orleans. He was banished from Paris and imprisoned in the Bastille for nearly a year in 1717. While in prison, he wrote his first play, the tragedy *Oedipe*, which was a resounding success and established him as a writer.

He adopted the name Voltaire in 1718. After an argument with the Chevalier de Rohan, Voltaire was in trouble again and spent two years in exile in England.

Already attracted to the freedom of speech and thought tolerated in England, Voltaire learned English and associated with leading literary figures Alexander Pope, Jonathan Swift and William Congreve. He was particularly impressed by the work of John Locke and Isaac Newton. His writing became gradually more philosophical, culminating in his *Lettres Philosophiques* (1734), a jewel of Enlightenment philosophy in which he expounds the principle that the goal of mankind is to achieve equality and happiness for all through the application of reason in science and the arts. He dismissed Blaise Pascal's goal of bliss attained through penitence and suffering. The *Lettres* set the tone for the progress of Western civilization and secured Voltaire's intellectual place amongst the French revolutionaries who would take up the fight only eleven years after his death. In some quarters, Voltaire has even been held responsible for the French Revolution!

The publication of *Lettres Philosophiques* caused an outcry, and a warrant was issued for Voltaire's arrest. He

took refuge in the chateau of the beautiful Madame de Châtelet where the two lived a sumptuous life steeped in culture. Their time together ended tragically when Madame de Châtelet died in childbirth in 1749 after an affair with the poet Saint-Lambert.

In 1758, Voltaire bought the estate of Ferney on the Franco-Swiss border. He spent the last twenty years of his life there, and it was where he wrote *Candide*. Voltaire died in 1778, a few months after his triumphal return to Paris. He was buried at the Abbey of Scellières shortly before the arrival of an order prohibiting his Christian burial. His remains are now in the Panthéon in Paris.

In his life and writings, he campaigned tirelessly for religious tolerance and the abolition of barbarous punishments. He argued for a theistic stance, in which simple worship supplants the complications and machinations of the church. Constantly speaking out against the abuses of the Church and civil authority, he was often in trouble – exiled, imprisoned and denounced. He battled, too, against the emerging Romantic movement in philosophy and literature.

Besides his philosophy and philosophical tales, Voltaire wrote poetry, plays, pamphlets and over 2,000 letters – and perhaps the first science fiction story. His tale *Micromégas* tells of two extraterrestrial beings who visit Earth. Though *Lettres philosophiques* and *Candide* have been constantly reprinted, most of Voltaire's other writings have slipped into obscurity.

Anne Rooney, Cambridge, 2009

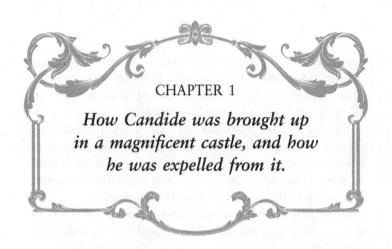

CHAPTER 1

How Candide was brought up in a magnificent castle, and how he was expelled from it.

In a castle in Westphalia, belonging to Monsieur the Baron of Thunder-ten-Tronckh, lived a youth on whom nature had bestowed the most gentle manners. His face was the mirror of his soul. He combined a true judgment with simplicity of spirit, which is the reason, I understand, that he was called Candide. The old servants of the family suspected him of being the son of the Baron's sister, by a good, honest gentleman of the neighbourhood, whom that young lady never wished to marry because he had been able to prove only seventy-one quarterings, the rest of his genealogical tree having been lost through the injuries of time.

The Baron was one of the most powerful lords in Westphalia, for his castle had a gate and windows. There was even a tapestry hanging in his great hall. His farmyard dogs formed a hunting pack when needed, his grooms doubled as huntsmen, and the curate of the village served as his grand almoner. They all called him 'My Lord', and laughed when he told stories.

The Baron's lady weighed about three hundred and fifty pounds, and was therefore a person of great consideration, and she performed the honours of the house with a dignity that commanded still greater respect. Her daughter Cunégonde was seventeen years old, rosy-cheeked, fresh, plump and desirable. The Baron's son seemed to be in every respect worthy of his father. The Preceptor Pangloss[2] was the oracle of the family, and little Candide listened to his lessons with all the good faith of his age and character.

Pangloss was professor of metaphysico-theologico-cosmolo-nigology. He could prove admirably that there is no effect without a cause and that, in this best of all possible worlds, the Baron's castle was the most magnificent of castles, and his Lady the best of all possible baronesses.

'It is proven', he said, 'that things cannot be otherwise than as they are; for all being created for an end, all is necessarily for the best end. Observe, that noses have been formed to carry spectacles, so we have spectacles. Legs are visibly designed for breeches and we wear breeches. Stones were made to be carved and to build castles, therefore My Lord has a magnificent castle – for the greatest baron in the province ought to have the best residence; pigs were made to be eaten, therefore we eat pork all the year round. So those who have asserted that all is well were talking nonsense, they should have said that all is for the best.'

Candide listened attentively and believed innocently. Because he found Miss Cunégonde extremely beautiful, though he never had the courage to tell her so, he concluded that after the great fortune of being born Baron of Thunder-ten-Tronckh, the second degree of happiness was to be Miss Cunégonde, the third that of seeing her every day, and the fourth that of listening to Master Pangloss, the greatest philosopher of the whole province, and consequently of the whole world.

One day Cunégonde, while walking near the castle in a little wood that they called 'the park', saw Doctor Pangloss behind the bushes, giving a lesson in experimental physics to her mother's chambermaid, a pretty and very obliging little brunette. As Miss Cunégonde took a great interest in science,

---

2   The name Pangloss derives from two Greek words signifying 'all' and 'language'.

she breathlessly observed these repeated experiments. She saw clearly the force of the Doctor's reasons, the effects, and the causes. She turned back greatly flurried, thoughtful, and filled with the desire to learn, dreaming that she might well be a sufficient reason for young Candide, and he for her.

She met Candide on reaching the castle and blushed; Candide blushed also. She wished him good-day in a faltering tone, and Candide spoke to her without knowing what he said. The next day after dinner, as they left the table, Cunégonde and Candide found themselves behind a screen. Cunégonde let fall her handkerchief, Candide picked it up, she took him innocently by the hand, the young man innocently kissed the young woman's hand with particular ardour, sensitivity and grace; their lips met, their eyes sparkled, their knees trembled, their hands strayed. Monsieur the Baron Thunder-ten-Tronckh passed near the screen and, beholding this cause and effect, chased Candide from the castle with great kicks on the backside. Cunégonde fainted away; as soon as she came to she was slapped by the Baroness, and all was consternation in this most magnificent and agreeable of all possible castles.

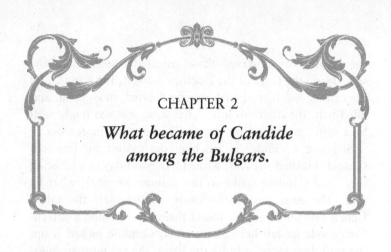

CHAPTER 2

What became of Candide among the Bulgars.

Candide, driven from terrestrial paradise, walked for a long time without knowing where, weeping, raising his eyes to heaven, turning them often towards the most magnificent of castles where the most beautiful of Baron's daughters was imprisoned. He lay down to sleep without supper, in the middle of a field between two furrows; the snow fell in large flakes. The next day Candide, frozen stiff, dragged himself towards the neighbouring town, which was called Waldberghoff-trarbk-dikdorff. With no money, dying of hunger and fatigue, he stopped sorrowfully at the door of an inn. Two men dressed in blue noticed him. 'Comrade,' said one to the other, 'now there is a well-built young fellow, and he is of the required height.' They went up to Candide and very civilly invited him to dinner. 'Gentlemen,' replied Candide with a most engaging modesty, 'you do me great honour, but I have no money to pay my share.' – 'Oh, sir,' said one of the blues to him, 'people of your appearance and of your merit never pay anything: are you not five feet five inches tall?' – 'Yes, sir, that is my height,' answered he, making a low bow. 'Then come, sir, take a seat; not only will we pay your share, but we will never suffer such a man as you to want money; men are born only to assist one another.' – 'You are right,' said Candide; 'this is what Pangloss always

taught me, and I see plainly that everything is for the best.'
They asked him to accept a few crowns, he took them and
offered to pay his bill; they refused; then they all sat down
at the table. 'Are you fervent in your love?' – 'Oh yes,' he
replied, 'I love Miss Cunégonde with all my heart.' – 'No,'
said one of the gentlemen, 'we are asking if you deeply love
the King of the Bulgars?' – 'Not at all,' he replied, 'because
I have never seen him.' – 'What?! He is the best of kings,
and we must drink his health.'

'Oh! Very willingly, gentlemen,' and he drank. 'That's it
then,' they told him, 'now you are the help, the support, the
defender and the hero of the Bulgars; your fortune is made,
and your glory is assured.' And with that they clapped him
in irons and carried him off to the barracks. There he was
made to wheel about to the right, and to the left, to draw
arms, to lower arms, to aim, to fire, to quick-march, and he
was given thirty blows with a cudgel. The next day he
performed the exercise a little less badly, and received just
twenty blows; the day after that they gave him only ten, and
his comrades considered him a prodigy.

Candide, all stupefied, had not yet quite worked out that
he was a hero. One fine spring day he decided to go for a
walk, striding straight forwards, in the belief that it was a
privilege of the human, as well as of the animal species, to
make use of their legs as they please. He had not advanced
two leagues when he was overtaken by four other heroes
each six feet tall, who tied him up and carried him to a
dungeon. At a court-martial he was asked which he would
like the best, to be flogged thirty-six times by the whole
regiment, or to receive twelve balls of lead in his brain in
one go. In vain he maintained that human will is free and
that he chose neither one nor the other; he was forced to
make a choice. He determined, by virtue of the gift of God
called liberty, to run the gauntlet thirty-six times; he suffered
this twice. The regiment was composed of two thousand men;

for him this amounted to four thousand strokes, which laid bare all his muscles and nerves, from the nape of his neck right down to his rump. As they were going to proceed to a third whipping, Candide, unable to bear any more, begged that they would be so good as to shoot him. He was granted this favour; they blindfolded him and made him kneel down. The King of the Bulgars passed at this moment and inquired as to the nature of the crime; and as he was a king of great genius, he understood from all that he learned of Candide that he was a young metaphysician, extremely ignorant of the things of this world, and he accorded him his pardon with a clemency which will be praised in all newspapers throughout the ages.

An able surgeon cured Candide in three weeks by means of ointments advised by Dioscorides.[3] He had already a little skin and was able to walk when the King of the Bulgars declared war on the King of the Abars.[4]

---

3   An ancient Greek physician of the time of the Roman emperor Nero.
4   The Abars were a tribe of Tartars settled on the shores of the Danube, who later lived in a region of Circassia.

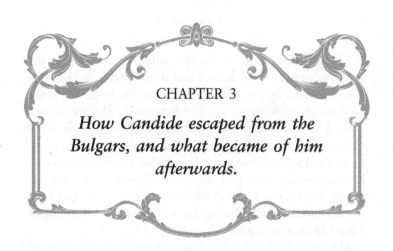

CHAPTER 3

How Candide escaped from the Bulgars, and what became of him afterwards.

There was never anything so gallant, so spruce, so brilliant and so well ordered as the two armies. Trumpets, fifes, hautbois, drums and cannon made such music as was ever heard in hell. The cannons first of all laid flat about six thousand men on each side; then the muskets swept away from this best of worlds nine or ten thousand ruffians who infested its surface. Next, the bayonet was sufficient reason for the death of several thousand more. The total might have amounted to about thirty thousand souls. Candide, who trembled like a philosopher, hid himself as well as he could during this heroic butchery.

At last, while the two kings commanded *Te Deum*s to be sung in their respective camps, Candide resolved to go and reason about effects and causes elsewhere. He passed over heaps of dead and dying, and first reached a neighbouring village; it was in cinders: it was an Abar village that the Bulgars had burnt, in accordance with international rights laws. Here old men riddled with bullets watched as their wives, with their throats cut, died while clasping their children to their bloody breasts. There, disembowelled girls were breathing their last after satisfying the natural desires of Bulgar heroes while others, half incinerated, begged to be finished off. Brains were strewn across the ground among severed arms and legs.

Candide fled quickly to another village; it belonged to the Bulgars, and the Abar heroes had dealt with it in the same way. Candide, by continuously walking over twitching limbs or through ruins, arrived at last beyond the theatre of war, with a few provisions in his knapsack, and with Miss Cunégonde still in his heart. His provisions failed him when he was in Holland; but having heard that everybody was rich in that country, and that they were Christians, he did not doubt that he would be treated just as well as he had been in the Baron's castle, before he was evicted on account of Miss Cunégonde's beautiful eyes.

He asked alms of several solemn-looking people, who all replied that if he continued to practise this trade he would be locked up in a house of correction where he would be taught how to earn his living.

Then he addressed a man who had been lecturing a large assembly for a whole hour on the subject of charity. But the orator, looking at him askance, said: 'What are you doing here? Are you here for the good cause?' – 'There is no effect without a cause,' Candide replied modestly, 'for everything is necessarily connected and arranged for the best. It was necessary for me to be banished from the presence of Miss Cunégonde, and then to run the gauntlet, and now it is necessary that I should beg my bread until I can earn it; none of this could be otherwise.' – 'My friend,' the orator said to him, 'do you believe that the Pope is the Antichrist?' – 'I have not heard it said that he is,' answered Candide; 'but whether he is or not, I need some bread.' – 'You do not deserve to eat,' said the other. 'Be off with you, rogue; be off with you, wretch; never approach me again.' The orator's wife, putting her head out of the window, and espying a man who doubted whether the Pope was the Antichrist, emptied over his head a full... Heavens above! To what excess does religious zeal carry ladies!

A man who had never been christened, a good Anabaptist called James, witnessed this cruel and ignominious treatment of one of his brothers, a two-legged creature with no feathers and a soul. He took him home, cleaned him up, gave him bread and beer, presented him with two florins, and even wanted to apprentice him in the manufacture of those Persian fabrics that are made in Holland. Candide, almost falling at his feet, exclaimed: 'Master Pangloss was right to tell me that all is for the best in this world, for I am infinitely more touched by your extreme generosity than by the harshness of that gentleman in the black coat and his lady wife.'

The next day, as he took a walk, he met a beggar all covered with scabs, his eyes without life, the end of his nose rotted away, his mouth distorted, his teeth black, choking as he spoke, tormented with a hacking cough, and spitting out a tooth with every spasm.

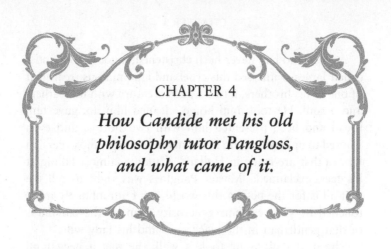

CHAPTER 4

How Candide met his old philosophy tutor Pangloss, and what came of it.

Candide, more moved by compassion than by horror, gave this revolting beggar the two florins that he had received from the honest Anabaptist James. The spectre stared at him, let fall some tears, and threw his arms around his neck. Candide recoiled in disgust. 'Alas!' said one wretch to the other, 'Do you no longer know your dear Pangloss?' – 'What do I hear? You, my dear master! You in this appalling state! What misfortune has befallen you? Why are you no longer in the most magnificent of castles? What has become of Miss Cunégonde, the most exquisite of girls and masterpiece of nature?' – 'My strength is failing me,' breathed Pangloss. Without further ado, Candide led him to the Anabaptist's stable, where he gave him a crust of bread to eat, and when Pangloss had recovered a little, he continued: 'So, what about Cunégonde?' – 'She is dead,' replied the other. At this word, Candide fainted; his friend revived him with a little sour vinegar which he happened to find in the stable. Candide opened his eyes again. 'Cunégonde dead! Oh, best of worlds, where are you? But what illness was it that killed her? Was it perhaps because she saw her father kick me out of his magnificent castle?' – 'No,' said Pangloss. 'She was disembowelled by the Bulgar soldiers, after being raped as much as is physically possible. They shattered the Baron's skull for attempting to defend her; the Baroness was cut into pieces; my poor pupil received the same treatment as his sister; and as for the castle, there is not one stone left standing, not an outhouse, not a sheep, not a duck, not a tree. But we have been well avenged, for the Abars have done exactly the same thing to a neighbouring barony belonging to a Bulgar lord.'

At this speech Candide fainted again; but when he came round, and when he had said all that it became him to say, he then inquired as to the cause and effect, as well as to the sufficient reason, that had reduced Pangloss to such a miserable state. 'Alas!' said the other, 'it is love; love, the comfort of the human species, the preserver of the universe, the soul of all sentient beings, love, tender love.' – 'Alas!' said Candide, 'I have known such love, that sovereign of hearts, that essence of our souls; yet it never earned me more than a kiss and twenty kicks on the backside. How could this beautiful cause produce in you an effect so hideous?'

Pangloss replied as follows: 'Oh, my dear Candide, you remember Paquette, that pretty maid who waited on the Baroness? In her arms I sampled the delights of paradise, which resulted in the hellish torments which devour me now; she was infected, and now she may be dead. Paquette had received this gift from a very learned Franciscan, who had traced it back to its source: he had had it of an old countess, who had received it from a cavalry captain, who owed it to a marchioness, who took it from a page, who had received it from a Jesuit who, while still a novice, had had it in a direct line from one of the companions of Christopher Columbus. As for me, I shan't give it to anybody, because I am dying.'

'Oh, Pangloss!' cried Candide, 'What a strange genealogy! Isn't the Devil at the root of it?' – 'Not at all,' replied the great man, 'it was indispensable to the best of worlds, a necessary ingredient: for if Columbus had not, on an island off the Americas, caught this disease which contaminates the

source of life, which frequently even prevents generation, and which is evidently opposed to the great end of Nature, we should have neither chocolate nor cochineal.[5] It should also be noted that up until now this disease has been specific to our Continent, just like religious controversy. The Turks, the Indians, the Persians, the Chinese, the Siamese, the Japanese, do not yet know it; but there is sufficient reason for believing that they will know it in their turn, a few centuries from now. In the meantime, it has made marvellous progress among us, especially in those great armies composed of honest, well-raised hirelings who decide the destiny of states; you can be sure that when an army of thirty thousand men fights another of an equal number, about twenty thousand on each side will have the pox.'

'Well, that is impressive!' said Candide, 'but you must be cured.' – 'And how will I do that?' said Pangloss. 'I don't have a penny, my friend, and nowhere in the world can you be bled or given an enema without paying, or without somebody paying for you.'

These last words decided Candide; he went and flung himself at the feet of the charitable Anabaptist James, painting so moving a picture of the state to which his friend was reduced that the good man did not hesitate to take Dr Pangloss into his house and have him cured at his expense. During the treatment, Pangloss lost only an eye and an ear. He still wrote well and understood arithmetic perfectly. The Anabaptist James made him his book-keeper. After two months, being obliged to go to Lisbon on business, he took the two philosophers with him aboard his ship. Pangloss explained to him how everything was arranged for the best. James was not of this opinion. 'It must be,' he said, 'that men have corrupted nature a little, for they were not born wolves, and yet they have become wolves. God gave them neither twenty-four-

---

5   An insect from Mexico, used to make scarlet dye for colouring food.

pound cannons nor bayonets, and yet they have made cannon and bayonets to destroy one another. I could add to this bankruptcies, and the courts which seize the property of bankrupts to cheat the creditors.' – 'All this is indispensable,' replied the one-eyed doctor, 'for private misfortunes make up the general good, so that the more private misfortunes there are, the greater is the general good.' While he reasoned, the sky darkened, the winds blew from the four corners of the earth, and the ship was assailed by a most terrible storm, within sight of the port of Lisbon.

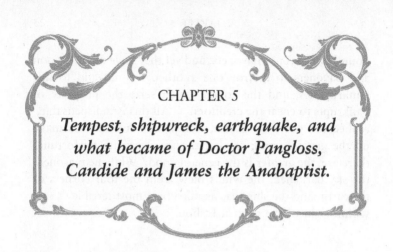

CHAPTER 5

Tempest, shipwreck, earthquake, and what became of Doctor Pangloss, Candide and James the Anabaptist.

Half the passengers were weakened, dying from that inconceivable anguish which the rolling of a ship produces in the nerves and in all the humours of the body as they are tossed in opposite directions; they did not have the strength to realize what danger they were in. The other half shrieked and prayed. The sails were torn, the masts broken, and the ship was gaping open. Those who could work did so, but no one could hear and no one was in command. The Anabaptist, on the upper deck, was helping with the rigging when a furious sailor struck him a violent blow and he went sprawling; but with the force of the blow he had let fly the sailor himself tumbled overboard, head-first. He remained suspended, stuck on a piece of broken mast. Honest James ran to his assistance, hauled him up, and in the effort fell into the sea in full view of the sailor, who left him to drown without even looking on.

Candide drew near and saw his benefactor, who rose above the water for a moment and was then swallowed up for ever. He was about to jump in after him, but was prevented by the philosopher Pangloss, who demonstrated to Candide that the Bay of Lisbon had been expressly created for the Anabaptist to drown in. While he was proving this *à priori*, the ship broke up and everyone perished except Pangloss, Candide and the brutal sailor who had drowned the virtuous

Anabaptist; the rogue swam safely to shore, while Pangloss and Candide were carried there on a plank.

As soon as they had recovered themselves a little they walked towards Lisbon; they had some money left with which they hoped to save themselves from starvation, after escaping the storm.

Scarcely had they reached the city, mourning the death of their benefactor, when they felt the earth tremble under their feet; the sea rose, boiling, in the harbour, breaking the vessels at anchor. Whirlwinds of fire and ash covered the streets and city squares; houses crumbled and roofs plummeted down on to foundations, and the foundations liquefied. Thirty thousand inhabitants of all ages and sexes were crushed under the ruins. The sailor, whistling and swearing, said: 'There's loot to be had here.' – 'What can the sufficient reason of this phenomenon be?' said Pangloss. 'This is the end of the world!' cried Candide. The sailor immediately ran off among the ruins, facing death to find money; found it, took it, got drunk, and having slept himself sober, purchased the favours of the first willing girl he met on the ruins of the destroyed houses, in the midst of the dying and the dead. But Pangloss caught him by the sleeve: 'My friend,' said he, 'this is not right, you are disobeying the law of universal reason and you have chosen your moment badly.' – 'Bloody hell!' replied the other, 'I am a sailor, born in Batavia;[6] I have trampled on the crucifix four times, on four voyages to Japan;[7] you've got the wrong man for your universal reason!'

Some falling bricks had wounded Candide; he was lying in the street covered with debris. 'Help!' he appealed to Pangloss, 'get me a little wine and oil; I am dying.' – 'This kind of earthquake is no new thing,' answered Pangloss,

---

6   A Dutch colony, now called Jakarta, in modern Indonesia.
7   Suspicious of the imperialist ambitions of the Christians, in the 1630s Japan expelled all foreigners, and European traders were forced to trample on the crucifix and renounce their faith.

'There were similar tremors in the city of Lima in America last year; the same cause, the same effects; there is definitely an underground seam of sulphur leading from Lima to Lisbon.' – 'Nothing is more probable,' said Candide, 'but for the love of God, a little oil and wine.' – 'How do you mean, probable?' replied the philosopher, 'I maintain that it is demonstrable.' At this point Candide lost consciousness, and Pangloss brought him some water from a nearby fountain.

The following day, having found some bits and pieces to eat amongst all the rubble, they recovered some of their strength. Then they worked alongside others to bring relief to those inhabitants who had escaped death. Some of the residents whom they had rescued gave them as good a dinner as they could in such disastrous circumstances. True, the meal was a cheerless one, and the guests watered their bread with tears; but Pangloss consoled them, assuring them that things could not be otherwise. 'Because,' he explained, 'all this is for the best, for if there is a volcano in Lisbon, then it cannot be anywhere else; it is impossible that things should not be as they are, for all is well.'

A little man dressed in black, an officer of the Inquisition, who was sitting at his side, politely spoke up: 'Apparently, Sir does not believe in original sin: for if all is for the best, then there has been neither Fall nor punishment.'

'I most humbly beg your Excellency's pardon,' answered Pangloss still more politely, 'but the Fall and curse of man played a necessary part in the best of possible worlds.' – 'Then Sir does not believe in liberty?' asked the officer. – 'Your Excellency will excuse me,' said Pangloss, 'but liberty can co-exist with absolute necessity, for it was necessary we should be free; for, in short, predetermined will ...' Pangloss was in the middle of his sentence when the officer nodded to his henchman, who gave him a glass of wine from Porto, or perhaps Oporto.

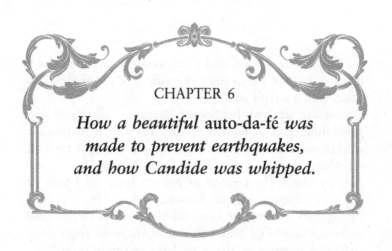

CHAPTER 6

How a beautiful auto-da-fé *was made to prevent earthquakes, and how Candide was whipped.*

After the earthquake that had destroyed three-quarters of Lisbon, the sages of the country could think of no more effective means of staving off complete ruin than to give the people a beautiful *auto-da-fé*; it had been decided by the University of Coimbra that the spectacle of a few people burning alive slowly, and with great ceremony, was an infallible secret to preventing the earth from trembling.

They had consequently seized a Biscayan convicted of marrying his godmother, and two Portuguese who had pulled the bacon garnish off a chicken they had eaten. After dinner, they came and tied up Doctor Pangloss and his disciple Candide; the one for speaking his mind, the other for having listened with an air of approbation. They were conducted separately to extremely cool apartments where they were never bothered by the sun; eight days later they were both dressed in *san-benito*s and their heads adorned with paper mitres. Candide's mitre and *san-benito* were painted with inverted flames and with devils that had neither tails nor claws; but Pangloss's devils had claws and tails, and the flames were upright. Dressed like this, they marched in procession, and heard a very moving sermon, followed by a fine droning chant. Candide was whipped to the rhythm of the singing; the Biscayan and the two men who had refused to eat bacon were burned, and Pangloss was hanged, although hanging was not the custom. The same day, the earth shook again with a terrific din.

Candide, terrified, bewildered, desperate, all bloody and palpitating, said to himself: 'If this is the best of possible worlds, what are the others like? I could have put up with the whipping, for I was whipped by the Bulgars; but oh, my dear Pangloss! The greatest of philosophers, did I have to see you hanged without knowing why? Oh, my dear Anabaptist! The best of men, did you have to be drowned in the harbour? Oh, Miss Cunégonde, the most exquisite of girls! Was it necessary that your belly be ripped open?'

He was turning away, barely able to stand, preached at, whipped, absolved and blessed, when an old woman approached him, and said:

'My son, take courage, follow me.'

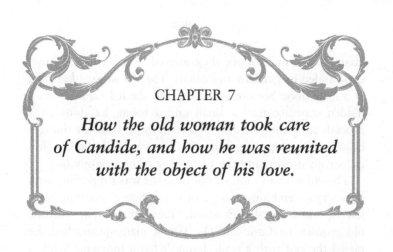

CHAPTER 7

*How the old woman took care
of Candide, and how he was reunited
with the object of his love.*

Candide did not take courage, but he followed the old woman to a hovel, where she gave him a pot of ointment to rub himself with and laid out something to eat and drink; she showed him a clean little bed, with a suit of clothes hanging next to it. 'Eat, drink, sleep,' she told him, 'and may Our Lady of Atocha, St Anthony of Padua and St James of Compostella watch over you; I will come back tomorrow.' Candide, still bewildered by all he had seen and all he had suffered and above all by the charity of the old woman, wished to kiss her hand. 'It is not my hand you must kiss,' said the old woman; 'I will be back tomorrow. Rub yourself with the ointment, eat and sleep.'

Candide, despite all his misfortunes, ate and slept. The next morning the old woman brought him his breakfast, inspected his back, and rubbed it with another ointment. Later on she brought him lunch; and in the evening she returned with his supper. The day after that she performed the same ceremonies. 'Who are you?' Candide kept asking her. 'Who has inspired you with so much goodness? How can I repay you?' The good woman never answered; she returned in the evening without bringing any supper. 'Come with me,' she said, 'and don't say a word.' She took him by the arm, and walked with him into the countryside for a quarter of a mile or so; they arrived at a secluded house, surrounded by gardens and canals. The old woman knocked at a little door. Someone opened, and she led Candide up a hidden staircase into a small gilded room, left him on a brocade sofa, shut the door and went away. Candide thought he was dreaming, imagining that his whole life had been a disastrous dream, and the present moment a happy one.

The old woman soon reappeared; she was supporting with difficulty a trembling woman, of stately figure, sparkling with jewels, and covered with a veil. 'Take off the veil,' said the old woman to Candide. The young man approached, he raised the veil with a timid hand. What a moment! What a surprise! He thought he could see Miss Cunégonde; indeed he could see her, for it was her. His strength failed him, he couldn't utter a word, he fell at her feet. Cunégonde fell on the sofa. The old woman poured spirits down their throats; they came round, they talked to each other: at first with broken voices, with questions and answers at cross purposes, with sighs, tears and ejaculations. The old woman advised them to make less noise and then left them to themselves. 'Is it really you?' said Candide. 'You're alive! And I find you in Portugal! So you were not raped then? They didn't rip open your belly as Doctor Pangloss assured me was the case?' – 'Yes, they did,' said the beautiful Cunégonde; 'but those two mishaps are not always fatal.' – 'But your father and mother were killed?' – 'That is only too true,' answered Cunégonde, in tears. – 'And your brother?' – 'My brother was also killed.' – 'And why are you in Portugal? And how did you know that I was here? And by what strange means did you have me brought to this house?' – 'I will tell you all that,' replied the lady, 'but first you must tell me everything that has happened to you since the innocent kiss you gave me and the kicks which you received.'

Candide obeyed her with a deep respect and, although he was bewildered, although his voice was feeble and trembling,

although his back was still hurting a bit, he nevertheless gave her a most honest account of everything that had befallen him from the moment they were separated. Cunégonde raised her eyes to heaven, and shed tears over the deaths of the good Anabaptist and of Pangloss; after which she spoke as follows to Candide, who did not miss a word, and devoured her with his eyes.

CHAPTER 8
Cunégonde's story.

'I was in bed and fast asleep when it pleased God to send the Bulgars to our delightful castle of Thunder-ten-Tronckh; they cut the throats of my father and my brother, and cut my mother into pieces. A huge Bulgar, six feet tall, seeing that I had fainted away at the sight of all of this, began to rape me; this made me come round, I regained my senses, I cried out, I struggled, I bit, I scratched, I wanted to tear the eyes out of this big Bulgar's head, not realizing that everything happening at my father's house was usual practice. The brute stabbed me in the left side and there is still a scar.' – 'Ah! I hope I shall see it,' said the naïve Candide. – 'You shall,' said Cunégonde, 'but let us continue.' – 'Do go on,' replied Candide.

And she picked up the thread of her story: 'A Bulgar captain came in, saw me all bleeding, and the soldier not put off in the least by his presence. The captain flew into a rage at the lack of respect showed him by this brute, and butchered him over my body. He ordered my wounds to be dressed and took me to his quarters as a prisoner of war. I laundered the few shirts that he had, I did his cooking. I must admit he found me very pretty; and I won't deny that he was an attractive man, with a soft and white skin; but otherwise he wasn't very bright or learned and it was plain to see that he hadn't been

educated by Doctor Pangloss. After three months, having squandered all his money and grown tired of me, he sold me to a Jew by the name of Don Issachar who traded in Holland and Portugal, and who had a passion for women. This Jew became very attached to my person, but could not triumph over it; I resisted him better than I had the Bulgar soldier. An honourable woman may be ravished once, but her virtue is strengthened by it. Hoping to get me to surrender, the Jew brought me to this country house. Until now I thought that nothing could equal the beauty of the castle Thunder-ten-Tronckh, but I was mistaken.

'The Grand Inquisitor caught sight of me one day at Mass, eyed me up at length, and sent to tell me that he wished to speak on private matters. I was conducted to his palace, where I acquainted him with the history of my family, and he explained how much it was beneath my rank to belong to an Israelite. A proposal was then made to Don Issachar that he should give me up to his Eminence. Don Issachar, being the court banker and a man of credit, would not hear of it. The Inquisitor threatened him with an *auto-da-fé*. At last my Jew, intimidated, came to a deal whereby the house and I should belong to both men; the Jew should have Mondays, Wednesdays and the Sabbath, and the Inquisitor should have the rest of the week. It is now six months since this agreement was made. Quarrels have not been wanting, for they could not decide whether the night from Saturday to Sunday belonged to the old law or to the new. As for me, I have so far held out against both of them, and I think this is why they still love me.

'Finally, to avert the scourge of earthquakes, and to intimidate Don Issachar, his Eminence the Inquisitor was pleased to hold an *auto-da-fé*. He did me the honour of inviting me to the ceremony. I had a very good seat, and the ladies were served with refreshments between Mass and the execution. I was in truth overcome with horror at the burning of those two Jews and of the honest Biscayner who had married his godmother; but imagine my surprise, my terror, my turmoil when I saw, dressed in a *san-benito* and capped with a mitre, a figure that resembled Pangloss! I rubbed my eyes, I looked at him closely, I saw him hung; I fainted. Scarcely had I recovered my senses when I saw you, stripped naked: this was the height of all horror, consternation, grief and despair. I will tell you now, in all honesty, that your skin is whiter and more perfectly rosy than that of my Bulgar captain. The sight of it redoubled all the feelings which were overwhelming and devouring me. I cried out, and would have said, 'Stop, barbarians!' but my voice failed me, and my cries would have been useless. When you had been severely whipped, I asked myself: 'How is it possible that loveable Candide and wise old Pangloss should find themselves in Lisbon, the one to receive a hundred lashes, and the other to be hanged on the orders of the Grand Inquisitor, whose beloved I am? Pangloss must have cruelly deceived me when he said that everything in the world is for the best.

'Restless, distraught, sometimes losing my reason, and sometimes ready to die of weakness, my mind was overwrought with the massacre of my father, mother and brother, with the insolence of my wicked Bulgar soldier, with the stab that he gave me, with my servitude under the Bulgar captain, with my hideous Don Issachar, with my abominable Inquisitor, with the hanging of Doctor Pangloss, with the *Miserere* chant to which they whipped you, and especially with the kiss I gave you behind the screen the day when I saw you last. I praised God for bringing you back to me after so many trials and I charged my old woman to take care of you and to bring you here as soon as she could. She has performed her task perfectly; I have tasted the indescribable pleasure of seeing you again, of hearing you, of speaking to you. You must be famished, I have a big appetite; let us start with supper.'

They sat down to eat, and when dinner was over, they settled on the sofa described earlier; there they were when Signor Don Issachar, one of the masters of the house, arrived. It was the Sabbath day. Issachar had come to enjoy his rights, and to protest his tender love.

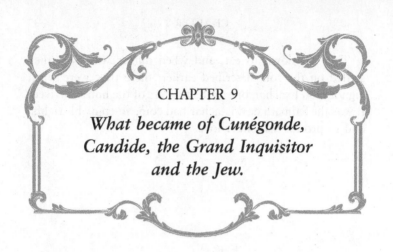

CHAPTER 9

What became of Cunégonde, Candide, the Grand Inquisitor and the Jew.

Issachar was the most quick-tempered Hebrew Israel had produced since the time of the captivity in Babylon. 'What?!' he said. 'You bitch of a Galilean, was the Inquisitor not enough for you? Must I share you with this rascal too?' As he spoke he drew a long dagger that he always carried with him and, not imagining that his adversary had any arms, he threw himself upon Candide; but our good Westphalian had been given a handsome sword by the old woman along with the suit of clothes. He drew his blade, despite his exceedingly gentle nature, and laid the Israelite stone dead on the tiles at Cunégonde's feet.

'Holy Mary!' she cried. 'What will become of us? A man killed in my apartment! If the police come we are lost!' – 'If Pangloss had not been hanged,' reasoned Candide, 'he would have given us good advice in this emergency, for he was a great thinker. In his absence, we had better consult the old woman.' The old woman was all for caution, and she had just started to give her opinion when suddenly another little door opened. It was an hour after midnight, the beginning of Sunday, and this day belonged to his Eminence the Inquisitor. He entered to see the flogged Candide, sword in hand, a dead man upon the floor, Cunégonde aghast, and the old woman giving advice.

Here is what passed through Candide's mind at this moment,

and how he reasoned: 'If this holy man calls for assistance, he will surely have me burned; he could do as much to Cunégonde; he has had me cruelly whipped; he is my rival; I have already started to kill him, so there's nothing to lose.' This reasoning was lucid and quick; so that without giving the Inquisitor time to get over his surprise, he pierced him through and through, and threw him down beside the Jew. 'Not again!' exclaimed Cunégonde. 'There'll be no forgiveness now; we are excommunicated, our last hour has come. How could you do it, you who were born so gentle, how could you slay a Jew and a prelate in two minutes?' – 'My beautiful young lady,' responded Candide, 'when one is in love, jealous, and has been flogged by the Inquisition, one stops at nothing.'

The old woman then spoke up, saying: 'There are three Andalusian horses in the stable and bridles and saddles too; the courageous Candide can get them ready. Madam has money and diamonds. Let's mount the horses quickly, although I can only sit on one buttock, and go to Cadiz; it has the finest weather in the world, and it is very pleasurable to travel in the cool of night.'

Candide immediately saddled the three horses. Cunégonde, the old woman and he travelled thirty miles without stopping. As they rode, the Holy Brotherhood entered the house; and they interred his Eminence the Inquisitor in a handsome church, and threw Issachar's body on a refuse heap.

Candide, Cunégonde and the old woman had by now already reached the little town of Avacena in the middle of the Sierra Morena mountains and were speaking as follows in an inn.

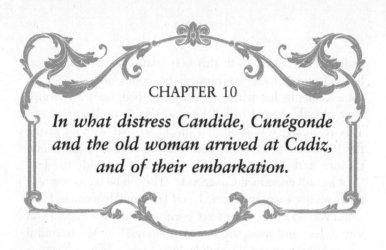

CHAPTER 10

In what distress Candide, Cunégonde and the old woman arrived at Cadiz, and of their embarkation.

'Who could have robbed me of my money and jewels?' said Cunégonde, in tears. 'How will we live? What shall we do? Where can I find Inquisitors or Jews who will give me more?' – 'Alas!' said the old woman. 'I strongly suspect that it was a Franciscan clergyman who stayed in the same inn as us last night at Badajoz. Heaven forbid that I should judge rashly, but he came into our room twice, and set out on his journey long before us.' – 'Alas!' said Candide. 'Dear Pangloss often demonstrated to me that the goods of this world are common to all men, and that each has an equal right to them. But according to these principles the Franciscan ought to have left us enough to complete our journey. Have you nothing left at all, my lovely Cunégonde?' – 'Not a penny,' she said. – 'What shall we do?' asked Candide. – 'Let us sell one of the horses,' replied the old woman. 'I will ride pillion behind Miss Cunégonde, although I can only balance on one buttock, and we will reach Cadiz.'

In the same inn there was a Benedictine prior; he bought the horse at a cheap price. Candide, Cunégonde and the old woman passed through Lucena, Chillas and Lebrixa, and finally arrived at Cadiz. There, a fleet was being prepared, and troops were being assembled to bring sense to the reverend Jesuit Fathers of Paraguay, who were accused of inciting one of the native tribes in a revolt against the kings of Spain and Portugal, near the town of San-Sacramento. Candide, who had served with the Bulgars, performed the Bulgar military exercise before the general of this little army with so much grace, speed, skill, pride and agility that he was given the command of an infantry regiment. He was a captain; he set sail with Miss Cunégonde, the old woman, two valets and the two Andalusian horses which had belonged to his Eminence the Inquisitor of Portugal.

During the entire crossing they reasoned incessantly on the philosophy of poor Pangloss.

'We are going to another world,' said Candide, 'and surely it is in this one that all is for the best. Because I must admit that one could moan a bit about what goes on in our world, physically and morally.' – 'I love you with all my heart,' said Cunégonde, 'but my soul is still full of fright at what I have seen and experienced.' – 'Everything will be fine,' replied Candide. 'The sea of this new world is already better than our European seas; it is calmer and the winds are more regular. It is certainly the New World which is the best of all possible worlds.' – 'God willing!' said Cunégonde. 'But I have been so terribly unhappy in my world that my heart is almost closed to hope.' – 'You complain,' the old woman said to them, 'but alas! You have not known such misfortunes as mine.' Cunégonde almost started to laugh, finding the good woman very amusing for pretending to be more unfortunate than she. 'Alas, my good woman,' she said, 'unless you have been raped by two Bulgars, been stabbed two times in the belly, had two of your castles destroyed, had two mothers and fathers cut to pieces before your very eyes, and seen two of your lovers flogged at an *auto-da-fé*, I do not see how you could be more unfortunate than I; added to which I was born a baroness of seventy-two quarterings – and now I have been put to work in a scullery!' – 'Young lady,' replied the old

woman, 'you do not know my birth; and if I were to show you my backside, you would not talk in that manner, and would suspend your judgement.' This speech excited a vivid curiosity in the minds of Cunégonde and Candide. The old woman spoke to them as follows.

CHAPTER 11
The old woman's story.

'I have not always had bleary eyes and red eyelids, my nose did not always touch my chin, and I have not always been a servant. I am the daughter of Pope Urban X and the Princess of Palestrina. Until the age of fourteen I was brought up in a palace, for which all the castles of your German barons could scarcely have served as stables; and one of my dresses was worth more than all the riches in Westphalia. I grew in beauty, grace and talent, in the midst of pleasures, admiration and high hopes. Already I was starting to inspire love, my breasts were developing and what breasts! White, firm and shaped like those of the Venus of Medici; and what eyes! What eyelids! What black eyebrows! The flames that shone from my eyes eclipsed the sparkling of the stars – or so the local poets told me. The women who dressed and undressed me used to fall into ecstasies, whether they saw my front or my behind; and all the men wanted to be in their place.

'I was engaged to the sovereign Prince of Massa Carara. What a prince! As handsome as I was, all puffed up with sweetness and charm, sparkling with wit and burning with love. I loved him as one loves for the first time – with adulation and transport. The wedding celebrations were prepared. There was great ostentation and unheard-of magnificence; there were non-stop festivities, parades and theatricals, and all Italy composed sonnets in my praise, not one of which was any good. I was almost at the peak of my happiness, when an old marchioness who had once been my Prince's mistress invited him over for a hot chocolate. He died in less than two hours in the most appalling convulsions. But that was just a trifle. My mother, in despair, and a lot less devastated than I was, wanted to get away from the fatal spot for a while. She had a very fine estate near Gaeta. We embarked on a local galley which was gilded like the great altar of St Peter's in Rome. And then a Salé pirate ship overwhelmed us and boarded the galley. Our men defended themselves just like the Pope's soldiers; they knelt down and threw away their arms, begging the pirates for absolution in *articulo mortis*.

'They were immediately stripped as bare as monkeys, as were my mother, our maids of honour and myself. It is remarkable with what diligence these men undress people. But what surprised me even more was that they thrust their fingers into the part of our bodies where we women never usually put anything but enemas. It seemed to me a very strange kind of ceremony; but everything seems strange when you have never left your country before. I soon learned that it was to see whether we had concealed any diamonds; it is a practice established since time immemorial among civilized nations that scour the seas. I found out that the religious Knights of Malta never fail to undertake this check when they capture Turks, of either sex; it is a legal right which is never neglected.

'I need not tell you how hard it was for a young princess and her mother to be taken to Morocco as slaves. You may well imagine everything we had to suffer on board the pirate vessel. My mother was still very handsome; our maids of honour, and even our waiting women, had more charms than are to be found in all Africa. As for myself, I was ravishing, I was beauty and grace personified, and I was a virgin. I did

not remain so long: this flower, which had been reserved for the handsome Prince of Massa Carara, was plucked by the pirate captain, an abominable negro, who thought he was doing me a great honour. Certainly the Princess of Palestrina and I must have been very strong to go through all that we experienced until our arrival in Morocco. But let us move on; these things are so common that they are not worth dwelling on.

'Morocco was swimming in blood when we arrived. The fifty sons of the Emperor Muley-Ismael each had their own following; this effectively resulted in fifty civil wars, of blacks against blacks, blacks against browns, browns against browns, and mulattos against mulattos. In short there was continual carnage throughout the empire.

'No sooner had we disembarked than some blacks from a faction opposed to that of my pirate turned up to rob him of his booty. After the diamonds and gold, we were the most valuable things he had. I was witness to a battle the likes of which you would never see in European climates. Northern peoples do not have hot enough blood, nor that raging lust for women that is common in Africa. It seems that you Europeans have milk in your veins; whereas it is vitriol, it is fire which flows through those of the inhabitants of the Atlas mountains and the neighbouring countries. They fought with the fury of the lions, tigers and snakes of that region to see who should have us. A Moor seized my mother by the right arm, while my captain's lieutenant held her by the left; a Moorish soldier had hold of her by one leg, and one of our pirates held her by the other. In a moment, nearly all our women were being pulled in this way by four soldiers. My captain held me concealed behind him; and with his scimitar in hand he killed everyone who challenged his fury. At length I saw all our Italian maids, and my mother herself, torn to pieces, cut up and massacred by the monsters who disputed over them. My companion slaves, those who had taken them,

soldiers, sailors, blacks, browns, whites, mulattos and even my captain, everyone was killed, and I was left dying on a heap of dead. Such scenes as this were taking place over an area of more than three hundred leagues, without anyone missing the five prayers a day ordained by Mahomet.

'With great difficulty I managed to extricate myself from that great heap of bloody corpses and crawled beneath a large orange tree on the bank of a nearby stream, where I collapsed with fright, fatigue, horror, despair and hunger. Soon afterwards, my overburdened senses gave themselves up to a sleep that was more like blackout than repose. I was in this state of weakness and unconsciousness, between life and death, when I felt myself pressed by something moving on my body. I opened my eyes and saw a white man, quite attractive, who was sighing and saying through gritted teeth: "*O che sciagura d'essere senza coglioni!*"[8]

---

8 'What a misfortune to be without balls!'

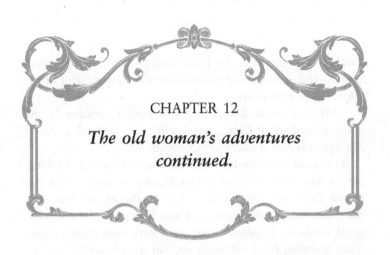

CHAPTER 12

The old woman's adventures continued.

'Astonished and delighted to hear my mother tongue, and no less surprised at this man's words, I answered that there were greater misfortunes than that of which he complained. I told him in a few words of the horrors which I had endured, and fainted a second time. He carried me to a neighbouring house, put me to bed, gave me food, waited upon me, consoled me, flattered me, told me that he had never seen anything as beautiful as me, and that he had never so much regretted the loss of what no one could ever give back to him.

'"I was born in Naples," he said, "where they castrate two or three thousand children every year; some die of the operation, others acquire a voice more beautiful than a woman's, and others are raised to offices of state. This operation was performed on me with great success and I was chapel musician to her Highness the Princess of Palestrina." – "To my mother!" I exclaimed. – "To your mother?" he cried, in tears. "What! Can you be that young princess whom I brought up until she was six, and who promised even then to be as beautiful as you are?" – "It is I, indeed; my mother is lying four hundred feet from here, torn into quarters, under a heap of corpses."

'I told him everything that had happened to me, and he related his adventures in turn. He told me how he had been sent to the king of Morocco by a Christian power, to conclude a treaty whereby the king was to be supplied with gunpowder, cannon and ships to help to demolish the commerce of other Christian governments.

'"My mission is done," said this honest eunuch; "I am going to embark at Ceuta, and I will take you back to Italy. *Ma che sciagura d'essere senza coglioni!*"

'I thanked him with tears of emotion; and instead of taking me to Italy he conducted me to Algiers, where he sold me to the Dey.[9] Scarcely was I sold, than the plague that had done the rounds of Africa, Asia and Europe broke out with great virulence in Algiers. You may have seen earthquakes, Mademoiselle, but have you ever had the plague?'

'Never,' answered Cunégonde.

'If you had,' continued the old woman, 'you would acknowledge that it is far more terrible than an earthquake. It is very common in Africa, and I caught it. Imagine the predicament of a Pope's daughter, fifteen years old, who in three months had suffered poverty, slavery, been raped almost every day, had seen her mother ripped into quarters, had endured famine and war, and was now dying of the plague in Algiers. In the end I did not die, but my eunuch, and the Dey, and almost the whole court of Algiers perished.

'When the initial fury of this gruesome pestilence was over, a sale was made of the Dey's slaves. A merchant bought me and took me to Tunis, where he sold me to another merchant, who sold me again in Tripoli; from Tripoli I passed hands to Alexandria, from Alexandria to Smyrna, and from Smyrna to Constantinople. At length I became the property of an aga[10] of the Janissaries, who was soon called to defend Azof against a Russian siege.

'The aga, who was a real gentleman, took his whole seraglio with him and installed us in a small fort on the

9 Dey (or bey): the pasha or governor of Algiers before the French conquest.
10 A Turkish military commander.

Palus-Méotides, guarded by two black eunuchs and twenty soldiers. The Turks killed prodigious numbers of the Russians, but the latter had their revenge. Azof was razed and its inhabitants slaughtered, neither sex nor age was spared, until only our little fort remained, and the enemy wanted to starve us out. The twenty Janissaries had sworn they would never surrender. The extremes of hunger to which they were reduced obliged them to eat our two eunuchs, rather than violate their oath. And after a few days they resolved to devour the women too.

'We had a very pious and humane Iman, who preached an excellent sermon to the Janissaries, exhorting them not to kill us outright.

"Why not cut just one buttock off each of those ladies," he said, "and you'll eat very well; if you have to come back for more, you can have the same again in a few days. Heaven will be grateful for such a charitable approach, and you will be saved."

'He was most eloquent; he persuaded them. The horrific operation was performed on us and the Iman applied the same balm to us as to children after a circumcision. We were all on the brink of death.

'Scarcely had the Janissaries finished the dinner with which we had provided them, than the Russians arrived in flat-bottomed boats; not one Janissary escaped. The Russians paid no attention to the condition we were in. There are French surgeons in all parts of the world; one of them, who was very skilful, took us into his care. He cured us, and as long as I live I shall remember that as soon as my wounds were healed, he propositioned me. What's more he told us all to take heart, assuring us such things happened all the time in sieges, and that the laws of war dictated it.

'As soon as my companions could walk, they were sent to

Moscow. I fell to the share of a boyar[11] who made me his gardener, and gave me twenty lashes a day. But after a couple of years this nobleman was broken on the wheel along with thirty other boyars for some intrigue at court, and I made the most of this opportunity and fled; I crossed the whole of Russia. For a long time I was servant at a tavern in Riga, then in Rostock, Vismar, Leipzig, Cassel, Utrecht, Leyden, the Hague and Rotterdam. I grew old in poverty and disgrace, with just half a behind, never forgetting that I was a Pope's daughter. A hundred times I was on the point of killing myself, but still I loved life. This ridiculous weakness is perhaps one of our most fatal characteristics; for what is more absurd than wishing endlessly to carry a burden that you want to throw down? To detest existence and yet to cling to it? In short, to caress the serpent which devours us, until it has eaten our very heart?

'In the different countries which it has been my lot to traverse, and in the inns where I have been servant, I have seen a vast number of people who held their own existence in abhorrence, and yet I only met twelve who voluntarily put an end to their misery: three negroes, four Englishmen, four Genevans and a German professor named Robek. I ended up as servant to the Jew Don Issachar, who placed me in your service, my fair lady. I attached myself to your destiny, and have been much more affected by your adventures than my own. I would never even have spoken to you of my misfortunes, had you not vexed me a little, and were it not customary to tell stories on board ships in order to pass the time. In short, Miss Cunégonde, I have had experience, I know the world. Why not enjoy yourself and ask each passenger to tell his story? And if there is no person among them who has not often cursed his life, who has not often thought himself to be the unhappiest of men, you can throw me headfirst into the sea.'

---

11 A member of the old Russian aristocracy.

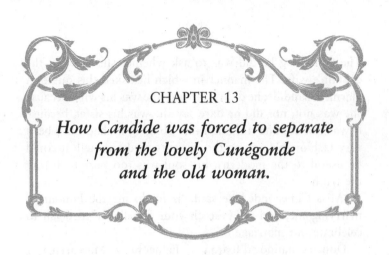

CHAPTER 13

How Candide was forced to separate from the lovely Cunégonde and the old woman.

The beautiful Cunégonde, when she heard the old woman's story, paid her all the respects due to a person of her rank and merit. She accepted her proposal and engaged all the passengers, one after the other, to relate their adventures. Finally, both she and Candide admitted that the old woman was right.

'It is a great pity,' said Candide, 'that the wise Pangloss was hanged, contrary to custom at an *auto-da-fé*; he would have lectured us admirably on the physical and moral evils that reign over earth and sea, and I should have felt strong enough to respectfully pose a few objections.'

While each passenger was recounting his story, the ship continued on its way. They landed at Buenos Aires. Cunégonde, Captain Candide and the old woman visited the Governor, Don Fernando d'Ibaraa y Figueora y Mascarenes y Lampourdos y Souza. This nobleman had a pride appropriate to someone with so many names. He spoke to people with such a noble disdain, carried his nose so loftily, raised his voice so mercilessly, assumed so imperious an air, and affected such a haughty manner that those who greeted him were strongly inclined to give him a beating. Cunégonde seemed to him the most beautiful thing he had ever seen.

The first thing he did was to ask whether she was not the captain's wife. The manner in which he asked this question alarmed Candide; he didn't dare say she was his wife, because she was not; nor did he dare say she was his sister, because it was not so; and although this obliging lie had once been very fashionable among the ancients, and although it could be useful to the moderns, his soul was too pure to betray the truth.

'Miss Cunégonde,' he said, 'is to do me the honour of marrying me, and we beseech your Excellency to deign to celebrate our marriage.'

Don Fernando d'Ibaraa y Figueora y Mascarenes y Lampourdos y Souza, twirling his moustache, smiled bitterly, and ordered Captain Candide to go and review his company. Candide obeyed, and the Governor remained alone with Miss Cunégonde. He declared his passion, insisting that he would marry her the next day with the blessing of the Church, or otherwise, however she preferred. Cunégonde asked for a quarter of an hour to review her situation, to consult the old woman, and to decide.

The old woman spoke as follows to Cunégonde:

'Mademoiselle, you have seventy-two quarterings, and not a penny. It is now in your power to become the wife of the greatest lord in South America, who has a very beautiful moustache; is it really for you to bother yourself with an inviolable fidelity? You have been raped by Bulgars; a Jew and an Inquisitor have enjoyed your favours: misfortune gives you certain rights. I admit that, if I were in your place, I should have no scruple in marrying the Governor and making Captain Candide's fortune.' While the old woman spoke with all the prudence that age and experience confer, a small ship entered the port carrying an *alcalde* and his *alguazils*,[12] and here is what had happened.

---

12 A judge accompanied by policemen.

As the old woman had already guessed, it was the Franciscan who had stolen Cunégonde's money and jewels in the town of Badajos, when she and Candide were fleeing. The friar tried to sell some of the diamonds to a jeweller, but the jeweller knew them to be the Grand Inquisitor's. Before he was hanged, the friar confessed that he had stolen them; he described the people he had stolen from and the route they had taken. The flight of Cunégonde and Candide was already known. They were traced to Cadiz, and then a vessel was immediately sent in their pursuit. The vessel was already in the port of Buenos Aires. The rumour was spreading that the *alcalde* was going to land, and that he was in pursuit of the murderers of his Eminence the Grand Inquisitor. The prudent old woman saw at once what was to be done. – 'You cannot run away,' she said to Cunégonde, 'and you have nothing to fear – it was not you who killed his Eminence – besides the Governor loves you and will not suffer you to be ill-treated: stay where you are.' She then ran immediately to Candide. – 'Flee,' she said, 'or in an hour you will be burned alive.' There was not a moment to lose; but how could he part from Cunégonde, and where could he find refuge?

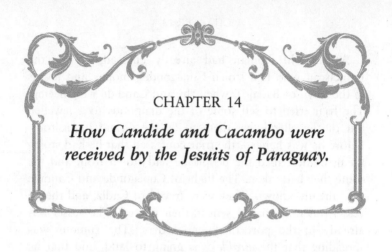

Candide had brought with him from Cadiz the kind of valet
that one often finds on the coasts of Spain and in the American
colonies. He was a quarter Spaniard, the son of a half-breed
in Tucuman;[13] he had been a choir-boy, sacristan, sailor,
monk, pedlar, soldier and lackey. His name was Cacambo,
and he loved his master because his master was such a good
man. He saddled the two Andalusian horses as fast as he
could. – 'Come, master, let's take the old woman's advice;
let's leave right away, and flee without looking back.' Candide
shed some tears. – 'Oh! My dear Cunégonde! Must I leave
you just when the Governor was going to celebrate our
wedding? Oh Cunégonde, what will become of you so far
from home?' – 'She will become what she can,' said Cacambo.
'Women are never at a loss, God provides for them, now
let's run.' – 'Where are you taking me? Where are we going?
What will we do without Cunégonde?' cried Candide. – 'By
St James of Compostella!' said Cacambo. 'You were going
to fight against the Jesuits; let's go and fight for them instead.
I know the road well, I'll take you to their kingdom, they
will be delighted to have a captain who knows the Bulgar
manoeuvres; you'll make a prodigious fortune. If you can't

---

13 A province of Paraguay.

make it in one world, then find another. It is a great pleasure to see and do new things.'

'Have you been to Paraguay before, then?' asked Candide. – 'Oh, yes!' replied Cacambo. 'I was kitchen servant at the College of the Assumption, and I know the government of *Los Padres*[14] as well as I know the streets of Cadiz. It really is an admirable government. The kingdom is more than three hundred leagues across and it is divided into thirty provinces. The Fathers own absolutely everything and the people nothing; it is a masterpiece of reason and justice. Personally I think there is nothing so divine as the Fathers, who make war on the kings of Spain and Portugal over here, and in Europe take confession from those same kings; who kill Spaniards over here, and in Madrid send them to heaven: this tickles me greatly. Let's push on; you are going to be the happiest of men. What a pleasure it will be for the Fathers to hear that a captain who knows the Bulgar drill has come to them!'

As soon as they reached the first checkpoint, Cacambo told the guard on duty that a captain wanted to speak to his lord the commanding officer. Notice was sent to the main guard. A Paraguayan officer ran and laid himself at the feet of the Commandant, to tell him the news. Candide and Cacambo were first stripped of their arms, and their two Andalusian horses were seized. The strangers were sandwiched between two lines of soldiers; at the far end stood the Commandant, with the three-cornered hat on his head, his gown hitched up, a sword by his side, and a spontoon[15] in his hand. He made a sign, and immediately twenty-four soldiers surrounded the newcomers. A sergeant told them they must wait, that the Commandant could not speak to them, and that the Reverend Father Provincial did not allow

14 'The Fathers', meaning the Jesuit rulers of Paraguay.
15 A short pike.

any Spaniard to speak unless he was there, or to stay more than three hours in the province. 'And where is the Reverend Father Provincial?' asked Cacambo. – 'He is on parade after celebrating mass,' replied the sergeant, 'and you cannot kiss his spurs for another three hours.' – 'But,' said Cacambo, 'Monsieur the captain, who is dying with hunger as I am myself, is not a Spaniard but a German; could we not have something to eat while we wait for His Reverence?'

The sergeant went immediately to pass this on to the Commandant. – 'Thank God!' said the Commandant. 'If he is a German, then I can speak to him: take him to my arbour.' Candide was taken at once to a summer-house decorated with a very pretty colonnade of green and gold marble, with trellis cages containing parrots, humming-birds, guinea-fowl and all the rarest birds. An excellent lunch was served up in bowls of gold; and while the Paraguayans ate maize out of wooden dishes, in the open fields and in the heat of the sun, the Reverend Father Commandant retired to his arbour.

He was a very handsome young man, with a full face, white, rosy skin, arched eyebrows, sparkling eyes, red ears, scarlet lips and a proud demeanour, but his pride was not that of a Spaniard or a Jesuit. Candide and Cacambo's arms were returned to them, as were the two Andalusian horses, to whom Cacambo gave some oats to eat just by the arbour, keeping an eye on them in case of surprise.

Candide first kissed the hem of the Commandant's robe, then they sat down to table. 'You are a German, then?' the Jesuit asked him in that language. – 'Yes, Reverend Father,' answered Candide. As they spoke they looked at one other with great amazement, and with such an emotion that they could not conceal. 'And from what part of Germany do you come?' said the Jesuit. – 'From the wretched province of Westphalia,' answered Candide. 'I was born in the castle of Thunder-ten-Tronckh.' – 'Heavens above! Is it possible?' cried the Commandant. – 'What a miracle!' cried Candide. – 'Is

it really you?' asked the Commandant. – 'It is not possible!' said Candide. They both fell backwards with surprise, they embraced, they shed streams of tears. 'What, is it you, Reverend Father? You, the brother of beautiful Cunégonde! You, who were slaughtered by Bulgars! You, the Baron's son! You, a Jesuit in Paraguay! I must confess this is a strange world that we live in. Oh, Pangloss! Pangloss! How happy you would have been if you had not been hanged!'

The Commandant dismissed the negro slaves and the Paraguayans who were serving them with drinks in goblets of rock-crystal. He thanked God and St Ignatius a thousand times; he clasped Candide in his arms and their faces were all bathed with tears. 'You would be even more amazed, more touched, and more beside yourself,' said Candide, 'if I told you that Miss Cunégonde, your sister, who you thought had been disembowelled, is in perfect health.' – 'Where?' – 'In your neighbourhood, at the house of the Governor of Buenos Aires; and I was coming here to wage war on you.' Every word they uttered in this long conversation added wonder to wonder. Their souls fluttered on their tongues, listened in their ears, and sparkled in their eyes. As they were Germans, they remained at the table a long time, waiting for the Reverend Father Provincial, and the Commandant spoke to his dear Candide as follows.

CHAPTER 15

How Candide killed the brother
of his dear Cunégonde.

'I shall never forget the dreadful day when I saw my father and mother killed and my sister raped. When the Bulgars had withdrawn, my dear sister could not be found, but my mother, my father and myself, with two maid-servants and three little boys, all of whom had been slaughtered, were put in a cart, to be taken for burial at a Jesuit chapel two leagues from our family home. A Jesuit sprinkled us with some holy water; it was horribly salty. A few drops of it got into my eyes and the Father noticed that my eyelid twitched a little; he put his hand on my heart and felt it beating. I was rescued, and after three weeks I was completely recovered. As you know, my dear Candide, I was very attractive. I became even more so, and the Reverend Father Croust,[16] the Superior of the House, conceived the tenderest friendship for me; he gave me a novice's robe, and some time later I was sent to Rome. The Father-General needed young German-Jesuit recruits. The sovereigns of Paraguay admit as few Spanish Jesuits as possible; they prefer foreigners since they believe them to be more obedient to their commands. I was judged fit by the Reverend Father-General to come and work in this vineyard. We set out – a Pole, a Tyrolese and myself. On my arrival,

16 A Jesuit known to Voltaire, with whom he quarrelled in 1754.

I was honoured with a sub-deaconship and a lieutenancy; now I am a colonel and a priest. We shall give a hearty welcome to the King of Spain's troops; I will answer for it that they shall be excommunicated and beaten. Providence has sent you here to assist us. But is it really true that my dear sister Cunégonde is in the neighbourhood, with the Governor of Buenos Aires?' Candide swore to him that nothing was more true, and their tears began afresh.

The Baron did not tire of embracing Candide; he called him his brother, his saviour. 'Ah! Perhaps, my dear Candide,' he said, 'we will enter the town as conquerors, and recover my sister Cunégonde.' – 'That is all I wish for,' said Candide, 'for I intended to marry her, and I still hope to do so.' – 'What insolence!' replied the Baron. 'You would have the impudence to marry my sister, who has seventy-two quarterings! I find you very impertinent to dare speak to me of such a reckless plan!' Candide, scared stiff by this outburst, answered: 'Reverend Father, all the quarterings in the world signify nothing; I rescued your sister from the arms of a Jew and of an Inquisitor; she owes me a lot, and she wishes to marry me. Doctor Pangloss always told me that all men are equal, and certainly I will marry her.' – 'We'll see about that, scoundrel!' cried the Jesuit Baron of Thunder-ten-Tronckh, striking him hard across the face with the flat of his sword. In an instant Candide drew his own sword and plunged it up to the hilt into the Jesuit's belly; but in pulling it out steaming hot, he burst into tears: 'Good God!' he said. 'I have killed my old master, my friend, my brother-in-law; I am the best-natured man in the world, and yet I have already killed three men, and two of them priests.'

Cacambo, who stood on guard by the door of the arbour, ran up. 'There's no choice other than to sell our lives as dearly as we can,' said his master to him, 'no doubt someone will come to the arbour any minute, and we must die sword in hand.' Cacambo, who had been in a great many scrapes

in his lifetime, did not lose his head; he took the Baron's
Jesuit habit and put it on Candide, gave him the square cap
of the dead man, and made him mount on horseback. All
this was done in the twinkling of an eye. 'Let's gallop, master,
everybody will take you for a Jesuit going to give orders,
and we will have passed the border before they can take
chase.' Even as he spoke he was on the move, crying out in
Spanish: 'Make way, make way, for the Reverend Father
Colonel!'

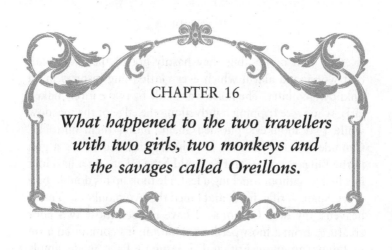

CHAPTER 16

What happened to the two travellers with two girls, two monkeys and the savages called Oreillons.

Candide and his valet had got beyond the barrier before anyone in the camp knew that the German Jesuit was dead. The wary Cacambo had taken care to fill his case with bread, chocolate, ham, fruit and a few bottles of wine. They penetrated into unknown country on their Andalusian horses, where they found no beaten track. At last they came to a beautiful meadow criss-crossed with streams. Here our two adventurers fed their horses. Cacambo suggested that his master have something to eat, and set him the example.

'How can you ask me to eat ham,' said Candide, 'after I have killed the son of Monsieur the Baron, and find myself doomed never to see the beautiful Cunégonde again in my life? What good will it do me to spin out my wretched days, if I have to live in remorse and despair, far away from her? And what will the *Journal of Trevoux*[17] say?'

As he spoke, he ate nonetheless. The sun was setting. The two wanderers heard some little cries which seemed to be uttered by women. They did not know whether they were

....
17 *Le Journal de Trevoux* was a Jesuit journal, published at Trevoux, that repeatedly attacked the *Encyclopédie* and Voltaire's involvement with it.

cries of pain or joy, but they hastily got to their feet with that worry and alarm which every little thing inspires in an unknown country. The noise was made by two entirely naked girls, who were tripping lightly along the edge of the meadow while two monkeys pursued them, biting their buttocks. Candide was moved with pity; he had learned to fire a gun in the Bulgar service, and he could have taken out a hazelnut in a hedge without touching a leaf. He took up his double-barrelled Spanish rifle, fired, and killed the two monkeys. 'Thank heavens, my dear Cacambo! I have rescued those two poor creatures from a most perilous situation; if I committed a sin in killing an Inquisitor and a Jesuit, I have made ample amends by saving the lives of these two girls. Perhaps they are young ladies of noble family, and this adventure could secure us great advantages in this country.'

He was going to continue, but stopped short when he saw the two girls tenderly embracing the two monkeys, breaking into tears over their bodies, and filling the air with cries of the utmost pain. 'I didn't expect to see so much good-nature,' he said at length to Cacambo, who answered him: 'Master, you have done a fine thing now; you have killed the lovers of these two young ladies.' – 'Their lovers! Can it be possible? You're joking with me, Cacambo, how can I possibly believe you?' – 'My dear master,' replied Cacambo, 'you are always surprised at everything. Why should you think it so strange that in some countries there are monkeys who obtain the favours of ladies; they are a quarter human, as I am a quarter Spanish.' – 'Alas!' replied Candide, 'I remember hearing Master Pangloss say that in the past such accidents used to happen, and that these liaisons produced *egipans*,[18] fauns and satyrs; that many great people of ancient times had seen them, but I took these stories to be myths.' – 'Perhaps now you will

---

18 Half-man, half-goat, *egipans* are deities worshipped by mountain dwellers which pay tricks on travellers.

be convinced', said Cacambo, 'that it is the truth, and you see how people behave who have not had a proper education. All I fear is that those ladies will get us into trouble.'

These sound reflections encouraged Candide to leave the meadow and to plunge into a wood. He and Cacambo ate there; and after cursing the Portuguese Inquisitor, the Governor of Buenos Aires and the Baron, they fell asleep on the moss. When they awoke, they felt as though they could not move. The reason for this was that during the night the Oreillons, who inhabited that country, and to whom the two ladies had denounced them, had tied them up with ropes made of the bark of trees. They were surrounded by fifty naked Oreillons, armed with arrows, clubs and flint axes: some were making a large cauldron boil, others were preparing spits, and all were shouting: 'It's a Jesuit! A Jesuit! We shall be avenged, we shall eat well, let's dine on Jesuit, let's eat him!'

'I told you, my dear master,' cried Cacambo sadly, 'that those two girls would land us in trouble.' Candide, seeing the cauldron and the spits, cried: 'We are certainly going to be either roasted or boiled. Ah! What would Master Pangloss say, if he saw how nature is really formed? Everything is for the best; that's as may be, but I admit it is very cruel to have lost Miss Cunégonde and to be spit-roasted by Oreillons.' Cacambo never lost his head. 'Do not despair,' he said to the distressed Candide, 'I understand a little of the language of these people, I will speak to them.' – 'Do not fail,' said Candide, 'to explain to them how frightfully inhuman it is to cook men, and how very unchristian.'

'Gentlemen,' said Cacambo, 'so you expect you are going to feast upon a Jesuit today? That is all very well; nothing is more just than to treat your enemies in such a way. Indeed, the law of nature teaches us to kill our neighbour, and such is the practice all over the world. If we Europeans do not exercise our right to eat them, it is because we have other

ways of eating well. But you do not have the same resources as we; certainly it is better to eat your enemies than to leave the fruits of your victory to the rooks and the crows. But, gentlemen, surely you would not want to eat your friends. You think that you are going to roast a Jesuit, but he is your defender, he is the enemy of your enemies that you are going to roast. As for me, I was born in your country; this gentleman is my master and, far from being a Jesuit, he has just killed one, and he is wearing his clothes; hence your misunderstanding of the situation. If you want to verify my story, take his habit and carry it to the first barrier of the Jesuit kingdom; inquire if my master did not kill a Jesuit officer. It will not take you long, and you can always eat us if you find that I have lied to you. But if I have told you the truth, you are too well acquainted with the principles and morals of international law not to pardon us.'

The Oreillons found this speech very reasonable; they dispatched two of their chiefs to inquire into the truth of the matter and the chiefs carried out their commission like men of sense, and soon returned with good news. The Oreillons untied their prisoners, showed them all sorts of civilities, offered them girls, plied them with refreshments, and conducted them back to the limit of their territories, proclaiming with great joy: 'He is not a Jesuit! He is not a Jesuit!'

Candide could not stop wondering at his release. 'What people!' he said; 'what men! what manners! If I had not been so lucky as to run my sword through Miss Cunégonde's brother, I would have been devoured without fail. But the state of nature is good after all, since these people, instead of eating me, showed me a thousand civilities, as soon as they discovered I was not a Jesuit.'

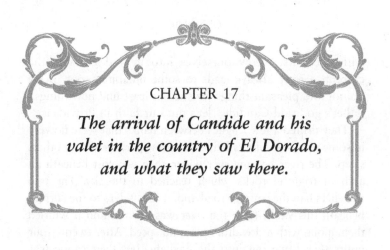

CHAPTER 17

The arrival of Candide and his valet in the country of El Dorado, and what they saw there.

When they reached the border of the Oreillon territory, Cacambo said to Candide, 'You see, this hemisphere is not better than the other one, take my word for it; let's go back to Europe by the shortest way.' – 'How could we get back?' said Candide. 'And where would we go? If I go to my country, I'll find the Bulgars and the Abars cutting everyone's throats; if I go to Portugal I'll be burned at the stake; if we stay in this country, we are in constant danger of being barbecued. But how can I resolve to leave the part of the world where my dear Cunégonde is living?'

'Let's head towards Cayenne,' said Cacambo. 'We'll find some Frenchmen there, they wander all over the world; they will be able to help us. Perhaps God will take pity on us.'

It was not easy to get to Cayenne; they knew more or less in which direction to go, but they came up against terrible obstacles of mountains, rivers, precipices, robbers and savages. Their horses died of fatigue; their provisions were finished; they fed for a whole month on wild fruits, and found themselves at last near a little river lined with cocoa trees, which kept them and their hopes alive.

Cacambo, who always gave as good advice as the old woman, said to Candide: 'We can't carry on, we have walked enough. I see an empty canoe on the riverbank; let's fill it with coconuts, throw ourselves into it, and go with the current; a river always leads to some inhabited spot. If we do not find pleasant things we shall at least find new things.' – 'Let's go,' said Candide, 'let's put our faith in Providence.'

They drifted a few leagues between banks that were flowery in some places, in others barren; in some parts gentle, in others steep. The river became ever wider, then was lost beneath an arch of frightful rocks which reached to the sky. The two travellers had the courage to abandon themselves to the current beneath this vault. Here the river was narrow and it whirled them along with a dreadful noise and speed. After twenty-four hours they came out into the daylight, but their canoe was dashed to pieces against the reef; they had to drag themselves from rock to rock for a whole league, until at length they discovered an extensive plain, bounded by inaccessible mountains. The country was cultivated as much for pleasure as for necessity; on all sides the useful was also the beautiful. The roads were covered, or rather adorned, with carriages of a glittering form and substance, carrying men and women of outstanding beauty, drawn by large red sheep[19] which were faster than the finest horses of Andalusia, Tetuan and Méquinez.

'Now this is a country', said Candide, 'which is better than Westphalia.' He and Cacambo went ashore at the first village they saw. Some of the village children, dressed in tattered golden brocades, were playing quoits at the edge of the settlement; our two men from the other world amused themselves by looking on. The quoits were large round pieces, yellow, red and green, which cast a singular lustre. The travellers picked a few of them off the ground; they were made of gold, of emeralds, of rubies – the least of them would have been the greatest ornament on the Mogul's throne. 'No doubt,' said Cacambo, 'these children playing quoits are the sons of the King of this country.' The village schoolmaster

---

19 These 'large red sheep' are most likely llamas.

appeared at this moment and called them to school. 'There,' said Candide, 'that must be the tutor to the royal family.'

The little truants stopped their game immediately, leaving the quoits on the ground with their other playthings. Candide gathered them up, ran to the schoolmaster, and presented them to him in a most humble manner, giving him to understand by signs that their Royal Highnesses had forgotten their gold and jewels. The schoolmaster, smiling, dropped them back on the ground, looked at Candide for a moment with a good deal of surprise, and went about his business.

The travellers took care to gather up the gold, the rubies and the emeralds. 'Where are we?' exclaimed Candide. 'The children of the kings of this country must be well brought up, since they are taught to despise gold and precious stones.' Cacambo was as surprised as Candide. At length they drew near the first house in the village; it was built like a European palace. A crowd of people were gathered about the door, and there were still more inside. They could hear delightful music, and there was a delicious smell of cooking. Cacambo went up to the door and heard the people were talking Peruvian, which was his mother tongue; for as everyone knows, Cacambo was born in Tucuman, in a village where no other language was spoken. 'I will be your interpreter,' he said to Candide; 'let's go in, this is an inn.'

Immediately two waiters and two girls from the inn, dressed in cloth of gold, and their hair tied up with ribbons, invited them to sit down to dine. They served four dishes of soup, each garnished with two young parrots; a boiled condor weighing two hundred pounds; two roasted monkeys of excellent flavour; three hundred humming-birds in one dish, and six hundred in another; exquisite ragouts; delicious pastries – all served up in dishes of a kind of rock-crystal. The waiters and girls poured out several liqueurs made from sugar-cane.

Most of the company were merchants and waggoners, all extremely polite; they asked Cacambo a few questions

with the utmost discretion, and answered his in a most obliging manner.

When as dinner was over, both Cacambo and Candide thought they could settle the bill by putting down as payment two of the large gold pieces they had picked up. The landlord and landlady burst out laughing and split their sides with mirth. At last they calmed down. 'Gentlemen,' said the landlord, 'it is clear you are foreigners in these parts, and we are unaccustomed to meeting your like. Forgive us therefore for laughing when you offered us the pebbles from our highroads to settle your bill. No doubt you don't have any local currency, but you don't need money to dine here. All inns established for the benefit of trade are paid for by the government. You have not eaten very well here, because this is a poor village; but everywhere else, you will be received as you deserve.' Cacambo translated this whole speech to Candide, who listened with the same admiration and astonishment as his friend showed in the telling of it. 'What sort of a country is this,' the one asked the other, 'that is unknown to the rest of the world, and where all nature is so different from ours? It is probably the country where all is well; for there absolutely must be somewhere like that. And, whatever Master Pangloss might say, I often found that things went fairly badly in Westphalia.'

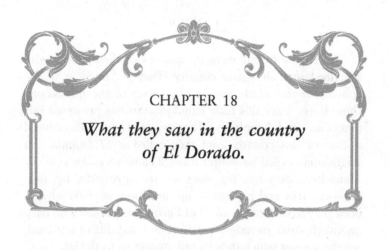

Cacambo expressed his curiosity to the landlord, who said to him: 'I am very ignorant, and happy with it; but in this neighbourhood there is an old man, retired from Court, who is the most learned person in the kingdom, and the most talkative.'

Straightaway he took Cacambo to the old man. Candide played a secondary role, and accompanied his valet. They entered a very plain house, for the door was only made of silver, and the panelling in the rooms was merely of gold, but so tastefully fashioned as to vie with the most opulent craftsmanship. The antechamber, in truth, was only encrusted with rubies and emeralds, but everything was arranged so well that it made up for such great simplicity.

The old man received the two strangers on a sofa stuffed with humming-birds' feathers, and presented them with liqueurs in diamond goblets; after which he satisfied their curiosity in the following terms:

'I am one hundred and seventy-two years old, and I learnt from my late father, equerry to the King, of the amazing revolutions of Peru, of which he had been an eyewitness. The kingdom where we are now is the ancient country of the Incas, who very imprudently left it in order to conquer another part of the world, and were at length destroyed by the Spaniards.

'More wise by far were the princes of their family who remained in their native country. They ordained, with the consent of the whole nation, that none of the inhabitants should ever leave this little kingdom; this has preserved our innocence and happiness. The Spaniards had a confused notion of this country, and they called it *El Dorado*. An Englishman called Sir Walter Raleigh came very near it about a hundred years ago. But since we are surrounded by inaccessible rocks and precipices, up until now we have always been sheltered from the greed of European nations, who have an unbelievable passion for the pebbles and dirt of our land, for the sake of which they would murder us to the last man.'

The conversation was long: it turned chiefly on the form of government in El Dorado, on customs, women, public entertainments and the arts. Finally Candide, who had always had a taste for metaphysics, made Cacambo ask whether there was any religion in the country.

The old man reddened a little. 'How could you doubt it?' he said 'Do you take us for ungrateful wretches?' Cacambo humbly asked what the religion of El Dorado was. The old man reddened again. 'Can there be two religions?' he said; 'We have, I believe, the same religion as all the world: we worship God night and morning.' – 'Do you worship just one God?' said Cacambo, still acting as interpreter to Candide's doubts. – 'But of course,' said the old man, 'because there are not two, nor three, nor four. I must confess that people from your side of the world ask the most extraordinary questions.' Candide was not yet tired of questioning the good old man; he wanted to know in what manner they prayed to God in El Dorado. 'We do not pray to Him,' said the worthy sage; 'we have nothing to ask of Him; He has given us all we need, for which we thank Him constantly.' Candide was curious to see the priests and asked where they might be found. The good old man smiled. 'My friends,' he said, 'we are all priests; the King and all the heads of

families sing hymns of thanksgiving solemnly every morning, accompanied by five or six thousand musicians.' – 'What! Have you no monks who teach, who argue, who govern, who conspire, and who burn people that are not of their opinion?' – 'We would have to be mad if we did,' said the old man; 'We all believe the same thing here, and we do not understand what you mean by monks.' Each of the old man's answers sent Candide into raptures, and he said to himself: 'This is very different indeed from Westphalia and the Baron's castle. If our friend Pangloss had seen El Dorado, he would no longer have said that the castle of Thunder-ten-Tronckh was the finest upon earth; it is evident that one must travel.'

After this long conversation, the old man ordered a coach and six sheep to be prepared, and freed up twelve of his servants to conduct the two travellers to Court. 'You will excuse me,' he said, 'if my age deprives me of the honour of accompanying you. The King will receive you in a manner that will not displease you, and no doubt you will make an allowance for the customs of the country, if some things should not be to your liking.'

Candide and Cacambo got into the coach; the six sheep flew, and in less than four hours they reached the King's palace, situated at the far end of the capital. The gateway was two hundred and twenty feet high and one hundred wide; but it is impossible to describe the material from which it was built. You can only imagine the prodigious superiority of these materials over the pebbles and sand which we call gold and precious stones.

Twenty beautiful damsels of the King's guard received Candide and Cacambo as they alighted from the coach, conducted them to the bath, and dressed them in robes woven of the down of humming-birds; after which the great crown officers, of both sexes, led them to the King's apartment, between two rows of musicians, a thousand on each side, as was the custom. When they drew near to the chamber of the

throne, Cacambo asked one of the great officers in what way he should pay his obeisance to his Majesty; whether they should throw themselves upon their knees or on their stomachs; whether they should put their hands upon their heads or behind their backs; whether they should lick the dust off the floor; in a word, what was the protocol? 'The custom', said the great officer, 'is to embrace the King, and to kiss him on each cheek.' Candide and Cacambo threw themselves round his Majesty's neck. He received them with all imaginable grace, and politely invited them to supper.

In the meantime they were shown the city. They saw public buildings as high as the clouds, market places decorated with a thousand columns, fountains of spring water, fountains of rose water, and fountains of liqueurs made from sugar-cane, all flowing continuously in the great squares, which were paved with a kind of precious stone that gave off a delicious fragrance like that of cloves and cinnamon. Candide asked to see the court of justice, the parliament; they told him there was none, and that there were never any lawsuits. He asked if they had any prisons, and they answered no. But what surprised him most and gave him the greatest pleasure of all was the palace of sciences, where he saw a gallery two thousand feet long, filled with instruments employed in mathematics and physics.

After rambling about the city the whole afternoon and seeing but a fraction of it, they were taken back to the royal palace. Candide sat down to table with his Majesty, his valet Cacambo, and several ladies. Never was there better food, and never did anyone show more wit than his Majesty at the dinner table. Cacambo explained the King's witticisms to Candide, and even when they were translated they were still witty. Of all the things that surprised Candide this was not the least.

They spent a month in this haven. Candide frequently said to Cacambo: 'My friend, I admit yet again that the castle where I was born is nothing in comparison with this country;

but after all, Miss Cunégonde is not here, and no doubt you have some mistress in Europe. If we stay here we shall only be the same as everyone else; whereas, if we return to our old world with just twelve sheep laden with the pebbles of El Dorado, we shall be richer than all the kings put together, we shall have no more Inquisitors to fear, and we can easily recover Miss Cunégonde.'

Cacambo was pleased with this idea. People so enjoy being on the move, getting noticed back home, and boasting of what they have seen on their travels, that the two happy men resolved to be happy no longer, but to ask his Majesty's leave to quit the country.

'You are making a mistake,' said the King. 'I know my kingdom does not amount to much, but when a person is comfortably settled somewhere, he should stay there. However, I certainly do not have the right to detain foreigners. That is a tyranny that neither our customs nor our laws permit: all men are free. You may go when you wish, but leaving will be very difficult. It is impossible to ascend that rapid river on which you miraculously arrived, which runs under vaulted rocks. The mountains which surround my kingdom are ten thousand feet high and as steep as walls; they are each over ten leagues wide, and there is no other way to descend them than by precipices. However, since you absolutely wish to depart, I shall give orders to my engineers to construct a machine that will transport you safely. When we have conducted you over the mountains no one can accompany you further, for my subjects have made a vow never to quit the kingdom, and they are too wise to break it. Otherwise you can ask me for anything you please.' – 'We ask nothing of your Majesty,' said Cacambo, 'but a few sheep laden with provisions, pebbles, and the earth of this country.' The King laughed. 'I cannot understand', he said, 'the taste you Europeans have for our yellow clay; but take as much as you like, and great good may it do you.'

He immediately ordered his engineers to construct a machine to hoist these two extraordinary people up and out of the kingdom. Three thousand skilled engineers went to work. The machine was ready in fifteen days, and did not cost more than twenty million pounds in the local currency. Candide and Cacambo were placed on the machine, as were two large red sheep saddled and bridled to ride upon as soon as they were beyond the mountains, twenty pack-sheep laden with provisions, thirty with presents of the curiosities of the country, and fifty with gold, diamonds and precious stones. The King embraced the two wanderers very tenderly.

Their departure, given the ingenious manner in which they and their sheep were hoisted over the mountains, was a splendid spectacle. Once they were on safe ground the engineers took their leave, and Candide had no other desire or aim than to go and present his sheep to Miss Cunégonde. 'We have,' he said, 'enough to pay the Governor of Buenos Aires, if Miss Cunégonde can be ransomed. Let's head towards Cayenne, take a boat, and then we can see which kingdom we can buy.'

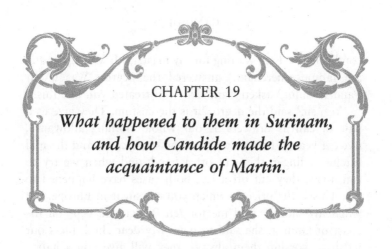

What happened to them in Surinam, and how Candide made the acquaintance of Martin.

Our travellers spent the first day very pleasantly. They were encouraged by the knowledge that they possessed more treasure than all Asia, Europe and Africa could scrape together. Candide, beside himself with joy, cut Cunégonde's name on the trees. On the second day two of their sheep plunged into a bog, where they and their burdens were lost; two more died of fatigue a few days later; seven or eight perished with hunger in a desert; and a few days later yet others fell down precipices. Finally, after travelling for a hundred days, they had just two sheep left. Candide said to Cacambo: 'My friend, you see how perishable are the riches of this world; there is nothing solid but virtue, and the happiness of seeing Miss Cunégonde again.' – 'Granted,' said Cacambo, 'but we have still two sheep left, with more treasure than the King of Spain will ever have; and in the distance I can see a town which I suspect is Surinam, belonging to the Dutch. We are at the end of all our troubles, and at the beginning of happiness.'

As they drew near the town, they came upon a negro stretched out on the ground, with only half his clothes on, that is, some blue canvas drawers. The poor man had lost his left leg and his right hand. 'Good God!' said Candide in Dutch. 'What are you doing here, friend, in such an appalling condition?' – 'I am waiting for my master, Mr Vanderdendur, the famous merchant,' answered the negro. 'Was it Mr Vanderdendur,' asked Candide, 'who treated you like this?'

'Yes, sir,' said the negro, 'it is the custom. They give us a pair of canvas drawers as our whole clothing allowance, twice a year. When we work at the sugar-canes and the mill catches a finger, they cut off a hand, and when we try to run away, they cut off a leg; both cases have happened to me. This is the price at which you eat sugar in Europe. Yet when my mother sold me for ten Patagonian ecus on the coast of Guinea, she said to me: "My dear child, bless our fetishes, worship them always; they will give you a happy life. You have the honour of being slave to our lords the whites, and in so doing you will make the fortune of your mother and father." Alas! I do not know if I made their fortune, but they certainly haven't made mine. Dogs, monkeys and parrots are a thousand times less wretched than us. The Dutch fetishes[20] who converted me declare every Sunday that we are all of us children of Adam – blacks and whites. I am not a genealogist, but if these preachers are telling the truth, we are all second cousins. In which case, as I'm sure you'll agree, it is impossible to treat one's relations in a more barbarous manner.'

'Oh, Pangloss!' cried Candide. 'You had not conceived of such an abomination: that's it, I must at last renounce your optimism.' – 'What is optimism?' asked Cacambo. – 'Alas!' said Candide. 'It is the madness of maintaining that everything is well when in fact it is not.' He shed tears over the fate of the negro, and weeping, he entered Surinam.

The first thing they inquired after was whether there was a vessel in the harbour that could be sent to Buenos Aires. For this they applied to a Spanish captain, who offered to make them an honest deal. He fixed a meeting at an inn,

---

20 The Dutch priests.

where Candide and the faithful Cacambo went to wait for him with their two sheep.

Candide, who always poured out his heart, told the Spaniard all his adventures, and confessed that he intended to elope with Miss Cunégonde. 'Then I will certainly not take you to Buenos Aires,' said the captain. 'I would be hanged, and so would you. The fair Cunégonde is my lord's favourite mistress.' This was a real blow for Candide; he wept for a long time, and at last he drew Cacambo aside. 'My dear friend,' he said, 'here is what you must do. Each of us has in his pocket five or six million in diamonds; you are cleverer than I – go and bring Miss Cunégonde from Buenos Aires. If the Governor causes any trouble, give him a million; if he still doesn't break, give him two. As you have not killed an Inquisitor, they won't suspect you. In the meantime I'll get another ship and go and wait for you in Venice; that's a free country, where there is nothing to fear from Bulgars, Abars, Jews or Inquisitors.' Cacambo applauded this wise decision. He despaired at parting from so good a master, who had become a close friend; but the pleasure of serving him prevailed over the pain of leaving him. They embraced in tears. Candide advised him not to forget the good old woman. Cacambo set out that very same day: he was an admirable fellow, this Cacambo.

Candide stayed on a while in Surinam, waiting for another captain to carry him and the two remaining sheep to Italy. He hired domestics and purchased everything necessary for a long voyage; finally Mr Vanderdendur, owner of a large vessel, came and offered his services. 'How much will you charge', Candide asked him, 'to take me straight to Venice – myself, my servants, my baggage and these two sheep?' The skipper settled on a price of ten thousand piastres; Candide did not hesitate.

'Aha!' said the careful Vanderdendur to himself. 'This stranger will give ten thousand piastres straight off! He

certainly must be rich.' Returning a moment later, he let him know that he could not undertake the voyage for less than twenty thousand piastres. 'Well then! You shall have them,' said Candide.

'Yes!' said the skipper to himself. 'This man agrees to pay twenty thousand piastres with as much ease as ten.' He went back to him again, and declared that he could not carry him to Venice for less than thirty thousand piastres. 'Then you shall have thirty thousand,' replied Candide.

'Well, well!' said the Dutch skipper once more to himself. 'Thirty thousand piastres are a trifle to this man; no doubt the two sheep are laden with an immense treasure. I won't press him further. Let him pay the thirty thousand piastres first, then we'll see.' Candide sold two small diamonds, the smaller of which was worth more than what the skipper was asking. He paid him in advance. The two sheep were put on board. Candide followed in a little boat to join the vessel in the harbour. The skipper seized his opportunity, set sail, and put out to sea, the wind favouring him. Candide, dismayed and stupefied, soon lost sight of the vessel. 'Alas!' said he. 'This is a trick worthy of the old world!' He returned to shore, overwhelmed with sorrow, because after all he had lost enough to make the fortune of twenty monarchs.

He went to the Dutch magistrate, and in his distress he knocked very loudly at the door. He entered and related what had happened, raising his voice more than necessary. The magistrate began by fining him ten thousand piastres for making a noise; then he listened patiently, promised to look into the affair as soon as the skipper returned, and ordered him to pay ten thousand piastres for the expense of the hearing.

This drove Candide to despair; he had in fact endured misfortunes a thousand times worse, but the coolness of the magistrate, and of the skipper who had robbed him, inflamed his bile and flung him into a dark melancholy. The

villainy of mankind revealed itself to him in all its ugliness, and his mind was filled with gloomy ideas. At last, since a French vessel was about to set sail for Bordeaux, and as he had no more sheep laden with diamonds to take along with him, he hired a cabin at a reasonable price. He made it known in the town that he would pay the passage and board – and give two thousand piastres – to any honest man who would make the voyage with him, on the condition that this man would be the most dejected and unfortunate person in the province.

Such a crowd of candidates presented themselves that a whole fleet of ships could hardly have held them. Since Candide wanted to select from the best, he picked out about twenty people who seemed to be fairly sociable, and who all claimed to merit his preference. He assembled them at his inn and gave them supper, on condition that each swore to relate his story truthfully. He promised to choose the man who seemed most worthy of pity and the most rightly upset with his circumstances, and to give some compensation to the rest.

The session lasted until four o'clock in the morning. Candide, as he listened to all their adventures, was reminded again of what the old woman had said to him on the way to Buenos Aires, and of her wager that there was not a person on board the ship who had not met with very great misfortunes. At every adventure related to him, he thought of Pangloss. 'Pangloss', he said, 'would have difficulty in proving his system now. I wish that he were here. Certainly, if all things are good, it is only in El Dorado and not in the rest of the world.' At last he chose a poor scholar who had worked ten years for the booksellers of Amsterdam, who judged that there was no other job in the world that could disgust one more.

This scholar, who was moreover a good fellow, had been robbed by his wife, beaten by his son, and abandoned by his

daughter who had been kidnapped by a Portuguese man. He had just been deprived of a small employment, on which he subsisted; and he was persecuted by the preachers of Surinam, who took him for a Socinian.[21] It must be admitted that the others were at least as wretched as he, but Candide hoped that the scholar would entertain him during the voyage. All the other candidates complained that Candide had done them great injustice; but he appeased them by giving one hundred piastres to each.

21 A disciple of Socin, a 16th-century radical Protestant.

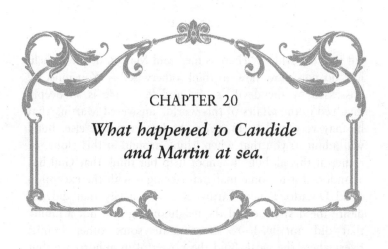

CHAPTER 20

What happened to Candide and Martin at sea.

So the old scholar, whose name was Martin, embarked with Candide for Bordeaux. Both had seen and suffered a great deal, and even if the vessel had sailed from Surinam to Japan, via the Cape of Good Hope, they would have had plenty to say to each other on the subject of moral and physical evil for the whole voyage.

Candide, however, had one great advantage over Martin, in that he still hoped to see Miss Cunégonde again, whereas Martin had nothing to hope for. What's more Candide had gold and diamonds. And, although he had lost one hundred large red sheep laden with the greatest treasure on earth, and although the villainy of the Dutch skipper still weighed on his mind, when he thought about what was still in his pockets, and when he spoke about Cunégonde, and above all at the end of a meal, he inclined towards Pangloss's doctrine.

'But you, Mr Martin,' he said to the scholar, 'What do you think of all this? What are your ideas on moral and physical evil?' – 'Sir,' answered Martin, 'the priests accused me of being a Socinian, but the truth is that I am a Manichean.'[22] – 'You are making fun of me' said Candide, 'there are no Manicheans

---

22 Manichaeism was a heretical religious system based on the dualistic conflict between good and evil.

left in the world.' – 'There is me,' said Martin, 'I cannot help it; I do not know how to think otherwise.' – 'You must be possessed by the devil,' said Candide. – 'He is so deeply involved in the affairs of this world,' answered Martin, 'that he may very well be in me, as he is everywhere else. But I will admit to you that when I look around at this globe, or rather at this globule, I cannot help but think that God has abandoned it to some malignant being – with the exception of El Dorado. I have hardly ever seen a city that did not desire the destruction of the neighbouring city, nor a family that did not wish to exterminate some other family. Everywhere the weak hold the powerful in abhorrence, but they cringe before them; and the powerful treat them like sheep whose wool and flesh they sell. A million regimented assassins, from one end of Europe to the other, pillage and murder under orders to make a living, for want of more honest employment. And even in those cities which seem to enjoy peace and where the arts flourish, the inhabitants are devoured by more envy, cares and anxiety than the victims of a town under siege. Private misery is yet more cruel than public calamities. In a word, I have seen so much and experienced so much that I am a Manichean.'

'Yet there is good in the world,' said Candide. – 'That may be,' said Martin; 'but I have not experienced it.'

In the middle of this argument they heard the noise of cannon. The din got louder every second. They each took out their spyglass. They saw two ships in battle, about three miles away; then the wind brought these ships so near to the French vessel that they had the pleasure of seeing the fight from a comfortable position. At last one of the two ships let off a broadside so low and accurately aimed that the other sank to the bottom. Candide and Martin could distinctly see a hundred men on the deck of the sinking vessel; they raised their hands to heaven and uttered terrible cries, and the next moment were swallowed up by the sea.

'Well,' said Martin, 'this is how men treat one another.'
– 'It is true', said Candide, 'that there is something diabolical
about this affair.' As he spoke, he saw something unidenti-
fiable, bright red in colour, swimming close to their vessel.
They put out the rowing boat to see what it could be: it was
one of his sheep. Candide was more joyful at recovering this
sheep than he had been grieved at the loss of a hundred laden
with the large diamonds of El Dorado.

The French captain soon saw that the captain of the victo-
rious vessel was a Spaniard, and that of the sunken vessel was
a Dutch pirate; it was the very same one who had robbed
Candide. The immense plunder that this villain had stolen was
buried with him in the sea, and the only thing to be saved was
the lone sheep. 'You see', said Candide to Martin, 'that crime
is sometimes punished. This rogue of a Dutch skipper has met
with the fate he deserved.' – 'Yes,' said Martin, 'but was it
necessary that all the passengers on his ship should die too?
God has punished the villain, but the devil drowned the rest.'

The French and Spanish ships continued on their way, and
Candide continued his conversations with Martin. They
argued for fifteen days in succession, and after fifteen days
they were no further advanced than on the first. But they
talked, after all, they communicated ideas, they consoled each
other. Candide caressed his sheep. – 'Since I have found you
again,' he said, 'I may well find Cunégonde.'

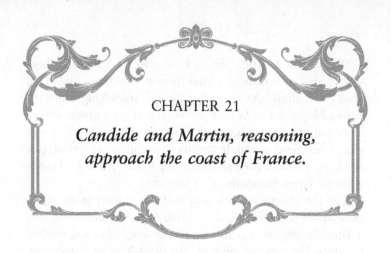

CHAPTER 21

Candide and Martin, reasoning, approach the coast of France.

At last the coast of France came into view. 'Have you ever been in France, Monsieur Martin?' asked Candide. – 'Yes,' said Martin, 'I travelled through several provinces. There are some where half the people are mad, some where they are too cunning; in others they are all quite weak and simple, in others they affect to be witty; but in all the regions, the principal occupation is making love, the next is slander, and the third is talking nonsense.' – 'But, Monsieur Martin, have you seen Paris?' – 'Yes, I have. All these kinds of people are found there; it is chaos – a confused multitude, where everybody seeks pleasure and where scarcely anyone finds it, at least that is how it seemed to me. I didn't stay long; on arrival I was robbed of all I had by pickpockets at the fair of St Germain. I myself was taken for a robber and thrown into prison for eight days, after which I served as a proof-reader of the press to earn enough money to return to Holland on foot. I met the writing rabble, the conspiring rabble, the fanatical rabble. It is said that there are very polite people in the city, and I would like to believe it.'

'For my part, I am not at all curious to see France,' said Candide. 'As I'm sure you can imagine, after spending a month in El Dorado, I no longer wish to see anything on earth apart from Miss Cunégonde. I am going to Venice to wait for her; we shall cross France on our way to Italy – would you care to accompany me?' – 'Most willingly,' said Martin. 'It is said that Venice is fit only for its own nobility, but that strangers meet with a very good reception if they have a good deal of money. I have no money, but you have, so I will follow you all over the world.'

'Talking of which,' said Candide, 'do you believe that the earth was originally a sea, as asserted in that large book belonging to the captain?' – 'I don't believe a word of it,' said Martin, 'any more than I do all the other fantasies that have been churned out lately.' – 'But for what end, then, has the world been formed?' said Candide. – 'To send us crazy,' answered Martin. – 'Are you not amazed', continued Candide, 'by the love which those two Oreillon girls had for the two monkeys which I told you about?' – 'Not in the slightest,' said Martin. 'I do not see what is strange about such a passion; I have seen so many extraordinary things that I have ceased to be surprised.' – 'Do you believe', said Candide, 'that men have always massacred each other as they do today? Do you think that they have always been liars, cheats, traitors, ingrates, brigands, weaklings, thieves, cowards, gluttons, drunkards, misers, envious, ambitious, bloody-minded, libellous, debauched, fanatical, hypocritical and fools?' – 'Do you believe,' said Martin, 'that hawks have always eaten pigeons when they have found them?' – 'Yes, I'm sure they have,' said Candide. – 'Well, then,' said Martin, 'if hawks have always had the same character, why should you believe that men have changed theirs?' – 'Well!' said Candide. 'There is a vast deal of difference, because free will...' Philosophizing thus, they arrived at Bordeaux.

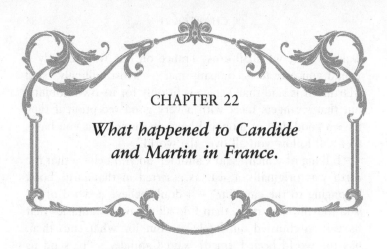

CHAPTER 22

What happened to Candide and Martin in France.

Candide only stopped in Bordeaux for as long as it took to sell a few of the pebbles from El Dorado and to hire a good coach with place for two passengers, for he could not leave without his philosopher Martin. He was only vexed at parting with his sheep, which he left to the Bordeaux Academy of Sciences, and which set as the question for that year's prize to find out why the sheep's wool was red. The prize was awarded to a learned man of the North, who demonstrated by A plus B minus C divided by Z, that the sheep necessarily had to be red, and die of the rot.

Meanwhile, all the travellers whom Candide met in the inns along the road said to him, 'We're going to Paris.' In the end, this general eagerness made him want to see the capital; and it was not so very great a detour from the road to Venice.

He entered Paris by the suburb of St Marceau, and fancied that he was in the ugliest village of Westphalia.

Scarcely had Candide arrived at an inn, than he came down with a slight illness, caused by fatigue. As he had an enormous diamond on his finger, and the people of the inn had noticed a prodigiously heavy box among his baggage, there appeared by his bedside two physicians that he had not sent for, some intimate friends who would not leave his side, and two do-gooders who warmed his broth. Martin said, 'I remember being sick in Paris too, during my first voyage; I was very poor, so I had neither friends, do-gooders nor doctors, and I recovered.'

However, what with all the medicines and bloodletting, Candide's illness became serious. A parish priest came to ask meekly for a note of confession payable to the bearer to the next world. Candide wanted nothing to do with it; but the do-gooders assured him that it was the new fashion; he answered that he was not a fashionable man. Martin wanted to throw the priest out of the window. The priest swore that they would not bury Candide. Martin swore that he would bury the priest if he continued to be troublesome. The quarrel grew heated; Martin took him by the shoulders and roughly threw him out, all of which caused a great scandal and a lawsuit.

Candide recovered, and during his convalescence he had very good company to dine with him. They gambled for high stakes. Candide was amazed that the aces never came to him, but Martin was not at all surprised.

Among those who paid their respects was a little Abbé from Périgord, one of those busybodies who are ever alert, officious, forward, fawning and complaisant; who watch out for strangers passing through, tell them the scandalous history of the city, and offer them pleasure at all prices. He first took Candide and Martin to the theatre, where a new tragedy was being performed. Candide found he was seated near some of the fashionable wits. This did not prevent him from crying openly at the perfectly acted scenes. One of the critics at his side addressed him during the interval: 'You are much mistaken in crying; that actress is terrible, the actor performing with her is worse still, and the play is worse than the actors. The author does not know a word of Arabic, yet the scene is in Arabia. Moreover, he is a man who does not believe in innate ideas; tomorrow I will bring you twenty pamphlets

written against him.' – 'How many dramas have been written in France, Monsieur?' Candide asked the Abbé. – 'Five or six thousand.' – 'What a lot!' said Candide. 'How many are any good?' – 'Fifteen or sixteen,' replied the other. – 'That is a lot.' said Martin.

Candide was most taken with an actress who played Queen Elizabeth in a somewhat insipid tragedy[23] performed from time to time. 'That actress,' he said to Martin, 'pleases me a lot; she has a deceptive air of Miss Cunégonde about her. I should be very glad to meet her.' The Abbé from Périgord offered to introduce him. Candide, brought up in Germany, asked what the etiquette was, and how they treated queens of England in France. 'You need to distinguish,' said the Abbé. 'In the provinces one takes them to an inn; in Paris, we respect them while they are beautiful, and throw them out with the rubbish when they are dead.' – 'Queens in the rubbish dump!' said Candide. – 'Yes, it's true,' said Martin, 'the Abbé is right: I was in Paris when Mlle Monime[24] passed, as the saying is, from this life to the other. She was refused what people call the "honours of sepulture" – that is to say, the honour of rotting with all the beggars of the neighbour-hood in an ugly cemetery. She was the only member of her troupe to be interred at the corner of the Rue de Bourgogne, which would have most upset her, for she was a woman of noble mind.' – 'That was very uncivil,' said Candide. – 'What would you have?' said Martin; 'These people are made thus. Imagine all the contradictions, all the incompatibilities possible – and you will find them in the government, in the law-courts, in the churches and in the public shows of this strange nation.'

'Is it true that people are always laughing in Paris?' said Candide. – 'Yes,' said the Abbé, 'but it's infuriating, because

23 This is an allusion to *Le Comte d'Essex* (1678) by Corneille (1625–1709).
24 A reference to Adrienne Lecouvreur (1692–1730), an actress and friend of Voltaire, who was refused a Christian burial.

they complain about everything with great bursts of laughter; they even do the most detestable things while laughing.'

'Who', asked Candide, 'is that great pig who spoke so ill of the play at which I wept, and of the actors who gave me so much pleasure?' – 'He is a bad character,' answered the Abbé, 'who earns his living by finding fault with every play and every book. He hates everyone who succeeds, like eunuchs hate lovers: he is one of the serpents of literature who nourish themselves on dirt and spite. He is a *folliculaire*.' – 'What is a *folliculaire*?' asked Candide. – 'It is a pamphleteer,' said the Abbé, '– a Fréron.'[25]

So ran the conversation between Candide, Martin and the Abbé from Périgord, as they stood on the staircase watching everyone go out after the performance. 'Although I am very eager to see Miss Cunégonde again,' said Candide, 'I should like to sup with Mlle Clairon, for she appears to me admirable.'

The Abbé was not the man to approach Mlle Clairon, who saw only good company. 'She is engaged for this evening,' he said, 'but I shall have the honour to take you to the house of a lady of quality, and there you will get to know Paris as if you had lived in it for four years.'

Candide, who was naturally curious, let himself be taken to this lady's house, at the end of the Faubourg St Honoré. The company was occupied in playing faro; a dozen melancholy punters each held a small hand of cards – a gloomy record of their misfortunes. A profound silence reigned; pallor was on the faces of the punters, anxiety on that of the banker, and the hostess, sitting next to the merciless banker, watched closely with lynx-eyes all the double-bets and all the increased stakes, as each player dog-eared his cards. She made them turn down the edges again with severe, but polite attention (she showed no anger for fear of losing her customers); this

---

25 Fréron (1718–76) was a journalist and critic of the *Encyclopédie*, an enemy of Voltaire.

lady called herself the Marquise of Parolignac. Her daughter, aged fifteen, was among the punters, and signalled with a covert glance the cheating of these poor people, who tried to repair the cruelties of fate. The Abbé from Périgord, Candide and Martin entered; no one rose, greeted them, or looked at them; all were profoundly occupied with their cards. 'The Baroness of Thunder-ten-Tronckh was more polite,' said Candide.

However, the Abbé whispered to the Marquise, who half rose, honoured Candide with a gracious smile and Martin with a most condescending nod. She gave a seat and a pack of cards to Candide, who lost fifty thousand francs in two games, after which they dined very gaily, and everyone was astonished that Candide was not dismayed by his loss. The servants said among themselves, in the language of servants:
– 'He must be some English lord.'

The supper was like most Parisian suppers: it started in silence, followed by a noise of indistinguishable words, then some pleasantries of which most were insipid, some false news, inferior reasoning, a little politics and a lot of malicious gossip; they even discussed new books. 'Have you read', said the Abbé from Périgord, 'the novel by Gauchat, Doctor of Divinity?'[26] – 'Yes,' answered one of the guests, 'but I have not been able to finish it. We have an abundance of impertinent writings, but all of them together do not approach the impertinence of "Gauchat, Doctor of Divinity". I am so fed up with the great number of detestable books that swamp us that I am reduced to punting at faro.' – 'And the *Mélanges* of Archdeacon Trublet,[27] what do you say of that?' asked the Abbé.

'Ah!' said the Marquise of Parolignac. 'The tiresome mortal! How he repeats what all the world knows as if it

26 An enemy of Voltaire and the *Encyclopédistes*.
27 Another enemy of Voltaire.

were interesting! How ponderously he discusses things that are not worth even lightly remarking on! How slavishly he poaches the wit of others! How he spoils what he steals! How he disgusts me! But he will disgust me no longer – it is enough to have read a few of the Archdeacon's pages.'

There was at table a wise man of taste who backed up the words of the Marquise. Then they talked of tragedies; the lady asked why there were tragedies that were sometimes performed on stage but which you could not bear to read. The man of taste explained very well how a play could be of some interest and yet have almost no merit. He proved in just a few words that it was not enough to introduce one or two of those situations which one finds in all novels, and which always seduce the audience, but that it was necessary to be new without being strange, to be frequently sublime, and yet always natural; to know the human heart and to make it speak; to be a great poet without letting anyone in the play appear to be a poet; to know language perfectly – to speak it with purity, with continuous harmony, without rhyme ever detracting from sense. 'Whoever', he added, 'does not observe all these rules can produce one or two tragedies that are applauded on the stage, but he will never be counted among the ranks of good writers. There are very few good tragedies. Some are merely idylls of well written and well rhymed dialogue; others are political arguments which send you to sleep, or pomposities that put you off; others are maniacal dreams written in a barbarous style, with broken speech, with long apostrophes to the gods, because they do not know how to speak to men, full of false maxims and bombastic commonplaces.'

Candide listened attentively to this speech and formed a very high opinion of the speaker, and as the Marquise had taken care to place him beside her, he leaned towards her and took the liberty of asking who this man was who had spoken so well.

'He is a scholar,' said the lady, 'who does not gamble, whom the Abbé sometimes brings to dinner. He is perfectly at home among tragedies and books, and he has written a tragedy which was booed off the stage, and a book which has never been seen outside his bookseller's shop, with the exception of one copy which he dedicated to me.' – 'What a great man!' said Candide. 'He is another Pangloss.'

So, turning towards him, he said: 'Sir, doubtless you think that all is for the best in the physical world and in the moral one, and that nothing could be otherwise than it is?' – 'I, Sir,' replied the scholar, 'think nothing of the kind. I find that everything goes awry; that no one knows either his rank, or his condition, what he is doing nor what he ought to do; and that except at supper, which is quite gay and where agreement generally prevails, the rest of the time is passed in impertinent quarrels: Jansenist against Molinist,[28] parliamentarians against the clergy, men of letters against men of letters, courtesans against courtesans, financiers against the people, wives against husbands, relatives against relatives – it is an eternal war.'

Candide replied: 'I have seen worse. But a wise man, who since has had the misfortune to be hanged, taught me that all is marvellously well; these are just the shadows on a beautiful picture.' – 'Your hanged man made fun of us all,' said Martin; 'the shadows are in fact horrible blots.' – 'It is men who make the blots,' said Candide, 'and they cannot avoid it.' – 'It is not their fault then,' said Martin. Most of the punters, who understood nothing of this language, drank, and Martin reasoned with the scholar, and Candide related some of his adventures to his hostess.

After supper the Marquise took Candide into her boudoir and made him sit upon a sofa. 'Well, then!' she said. 'So you are still desperately in love with Miss Cunégonde of Thunder-

28 Another word for a Jesuit.

ten-Tronckh?' – 'Yes, Madam,' answered Candide. The Marquise replied to him with a tender smile: 'You answer me like a young man from Westphalia; a Frenchman would have said, "It is true that I have loved Miss Cunégonde, but with you before my eyes, Madam, I fear I love her no longer."' – 'Alas! Madam,' said Candide, 'I will answer you as you wish.' – 'Your passion for her', said the Marquise, 'began when you picked up her handkerchief; I would like you to pick up my garter.' – 'With all my heart,' said Candide, and he picked it up. – 'But I would like you to put it back on,' said the lady, and Candide put it back on. 'You see,' said she, 'you are a foreigner. I sometimes make my Parisian lovers languish for fifteen days, but I give myself to you on the first night, because one must do the honours of one's country to a young man from Westphalia.' The beauty, having caught sight of two enormous diamonds on the hands of her young foreigner, praised them with such sincerity that from Candide's fingers they passed on to her own.

Candide, returning with the Abbé, felt some remorse in having been unfaithful to Miss Cunégonde; the Abbé sympathized with him. He had but a small stake in the fifty thousand francs that Candide had lost at cards, and in the value of the two brilliants, half given, half extorted. His plan was to profit as much as he could from the advantages that the acquaintance of Candide could procure for him. He spoke to him at length about Cunégonde, and Candide told him that he would certainly ask for forgiveness for his infidelity when he saw his beauty in Venice.

The Abbé became yet more polite and attentive, and took a tender interest in everything that Candide said, did, and wished to do.

'And so, sir, you have a rendezvous in Venice?' – 'Yes, Monsieur Abbé,' answered Candide. 'I absolutely must go there to meet Miss Cunégonde.' And so, carried away with the pleasure of talking about the object of his love, he related,

as he was wont to do, some of his adventures with the fair Westphalian girl.

'I believe,' said the Abbé, 'that Miss Cunégonde has a great deal of wit, and that she writes charming letters?' – 'I have never received any from her,' said Candide, 'for believe it or not, having been expelled from the castle on her account, I had no opportunity for writing to her. Soon after that I heard she was dead; then I found her alive; then I lost her again; now I have sent a messenger to her, two thousand five hundred leagues from here, and I am waiting for an answer.'

The Abbé listened attentively, and seemed a little distracted. He soon took his leave of the two foreigners after embracing them tenderly. The following day Candide received, on awaking, a letter couched in these terms:

Monsieur, my dearest love, for eight days I have been ill in this town. I learn that you are here. I would fly to your arms if I could but move. I was informed of your passage at Bordeaux, where I left faithful Cacambo and the old woman, who are to follow me very soon. The Governor of Buenos Aires has taken everything, but your heart remains to me. Come! Your presence will return the life to me, or kill me with pleasure.

This charming, unhoped-for letter filled Candide with inexpressible joy, and the illness of his dear Cunégonde overwhelmed him with grief. Divided between these two emotions, he took his gold and his diamonds and was driven, with Martin, to the hotel where Miss Cunégonde was lodged. He entered her room trembling with emotion, his heart palpitating, his voice choking; he tried to open the curtains of the bed to let some light in. – 'You can't do that,' said the servant-maid; 'the light will kill her,' and immediately she drew the curtain again. 'My dear Cunégonde,' said Candide, weeping, 'how are you feeling? If you cannot see me, speak to me at least.' – 'She cannot speak,' said the maid. The lady then put a plump hand out from the bed, and for a long time Candide

bathed it with his tears, and then filled it with diamonds, leaving a bag of gold upon the easy chair.

Into the midst of these transports came an officer, followed by the Abbé from Périgord and a file of soldiers. 'Are these', he asked, 'the two suspect foreigners?' He immediately had them arrested and ordered that they be carried to prison. 'Travellers are not treated like this in El Dorado,' said Candide. – 'I am more a Manichean now than ever,' said Martin. – 'But my dear sir, where are you taking us?' said Candide. 'To an underground dungeon,' answered the officer.

Martin, having recovered himself a little, guessed that the lady acting the part of Cunégonde was a cheat, that the Abbé from Périgord was a scoundrel who had abused Candide's innocence as soon as he could, and that the officer was another fraud whom they could easily get rid of.

Rather than expose himself before a court of justice, Candide, enlightened by Martin and impatient to see the real Cunégonde, proposed to the officer that he accept three small diamonds, each worth about three thousand pistoles. 'Ah, sir,' said the man with the ivory baton, 'had you committed every crime imaginable you would be the most honest man in the world. Three diamonds! Each worth three thousand pistoles! Sir, instead of carrying you to jail I would give my life to serve you. There are orders for arresting all foreigners, but leave it to me; I have a brother at Dieppe in Normandy, I'll take you there, and if you have a diamond to give him he'll take as much care of you as I.'

'And why are all foreigners being arrested?' asked Candide. The Abbé from Périgord now spoke: 'Because a poor beggar from the country of Atrébatie heard some foolish things said; this induced him to commit parricide,[29] not like that of May 1610 but like that of December 1594, and like many others

---

29 An allusion to the assassination attempt made by Damiens (from Arras) on Louis XV.

committed in other months and years by other poor devils who had heard nonsense spoken.'

The officer then explained what the Abbé meant. 'Ah, the monsters!' cried Candide. 'How can there be such horrors among a people who like dancing and singing! How can I get out of this country, where monkeys provoke tigers, as quickly as possible? I have seen bears in my own country, but I have seen no men anywhere except in El Dorado. In the name of God, officer, take me to Venice, where I am to await Miss Cunégonde.' – 'I can only take you to lower Normandy,' said the officer. Immediately he ordered the irons to be taken off, acknowledged himself mistaken, sent away his men, and took Candide and Martin to Dieppe, where he left them in the care of his brother. There was a small Dutch ship in the harbour. The Norman, who with the help of three more diamonds had become the most obliging of men, put Candide and his attendants on board this vessel that was about to set sail for Portsmouth in England. This was not the way to Venice, but Candide felt he was being delivered from hell, and he expected that he would soon have an opportunity for resuming the road to Venice.

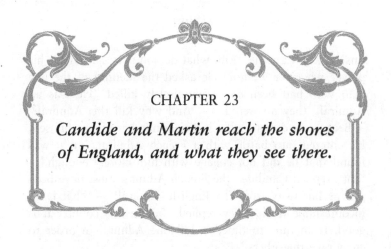

CHAPTER 23

Candide and Martin reach the shores of England, and what they see there.

'Oh, Pangloss! Pangloss! Oh, Martin! Martin! Oh, my dear Cunégonde! What sort of a world is this?' cried Candide on board the Dutch ship. – 'A mad and abominable one,' replied Martin. – 'You know England; tell me, are they as mad there as in France?' – 'It is another kind of madness,' said Martin. 'You know that these two nations are at war over a few acres of snow on the Canadian border,[30] and that they are spending much more on this beautiful war than Canada is worth. But to tell you precisely whether one country has more people who should be locked up than another, is something my imperfect intelligence will not permit. I only know that in general the people we are going to see are very ill-tempered indeed.'

Talking thus they arrived at Portsmouth. A crowd of people was assembled on the shore, engrossed in watching rather a large man, who was kneeling down with his eyes bandaged on the upper deck of one the ships of the fleet; four soldiers were stationed directly facing this man, they each fired three balls at his head with all the calmness in the world, and the whole assembly went away very well satisfied. 'What is all

---

30 The Seven Years' War (1756–63) was a widespread war between the European powers, during which England and France struggled over their colonial possessions in North America.

this?' asked Candide, 'And what demon is it that wields his power wherever we go?' He asked the identity of the fine man who had been so ceremoniously killed. 'He was an Admiral,' they answered.[31] – 'And why kill this Admiral?' – 'Because he did not kill a sufficient number of men himself. He entered into battle with a French Admiral, but it was found that he did not engage with him closely enough.' – 'But', replied Candide, 'the French Admiral must have been just as far away from the English Admiral!' – 'That is an incontestable truth,' they replied, 'but in this country it is good, from time to time, to kill one Admiral in order to encourage the others.'

Candide was so shocked and bewildered by what he saw and heard, that he absolutely refused to set foot on the shores of England, and he made a bargain with the Dutch skipper (not even caring if he were swindled as he had been in Surinam) to take him straight to Venice.

In two days, the skipper was ready. They skirted the coast of France; they passed in sight of Lisbon, and Candide trembled. They passed through the Straits of Gibraltar and entered the Mediterranean; at last they docked in Venice.

'God be praised!' said Candide, embracing Martin; 'It is here that I shall see my beautiful Cunégonde again. I trust Cacambo as I would myself. All is well, all will be well, all goes as well as it possibly can.'

31 A reference to Admiral John Byng, who was executed in 1757.

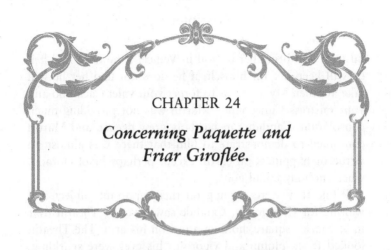

As soon as he arrived in Venice, Candide began searching for Cacambo in every inn, every coffee-house and every brothel, but to no avail. Every day he sent to inquire of all the ships and boats that entered the harbour, but there was no news of Cacambo.

'What!' he said to Martin, 'I have had time to travel from Surinam to Bordeaux, to go from Bordeaux to Paris, from Paris to Dieppe, from Dieppe to Portsmouth, to coast the length of Portugal and Spain, to cross the whole Mediterranean, to spend a few months in Venice, and still the beautiful Cunégonde has not arrived! Instead of her I have only met a Parisian hussy and an Abbé from Périgord. Cunégonde must be dead, and there is nothing left for me but to die. Alas! It would have been better to stay in the paradise of El Dorado than to come back to this cursed Europe! You are only too right, my dear Martin: all is but illusion and calamity!'

He fell into a deep melancholy, and neither went to see the fashionable opera, nor any of the other entertainments of the Carnival; not one woman tempted him in the slightest. Martin said to him, 'You must be very simple indeed if you believe that a half-caste valet, with five or six million in his pocket, will go to the ends of the earth to seek out your mistress and bring her to you in Venice. If he does find her, he will keep her for himself; if he does not find her he will take another. My advice is to forget your valet Cacambo and your mistress Cunégonde.' Martin was not providing much consolation. Candide's melancholy grew deeper, and Martin continued to demonstrate to him that there was almost no virtue or happiness on earth, except perhaps in El Dorado, where nobody could go.

While they were arguing on this important subject and waiting for Cunégonde, Candide saw a young Theatin friar in St Mark's square, holding a girl on his arm. The Theatin looked fresh, plump and vigorous; his eyes were sparkling, his air assured, his expression lofty, and his step bold. The girl was very pretty and she was singing; she gazed lovingly at her Theatin, and from time to time pinched his fat cheeks.

'You will at least admit', said Candide to Martin, 'that those two are happy. Up until now, around the whole habitable world, I have only met unfortunate people, except in El Dorado; but as to this girl and this Theatin, I wager that they are very happy creatures indeed.' – 'I wager that they are not,' said Martin. – 'Then we need only ask them to dinner,' said Candide, 'and you will see whether I am right.'

He approached them immediately, presented his compliments, and invited them to his hotel to eat macaroni, Lombard partridge and caviar, and to drink some Montepulciano and Lachrymæ Christi, as well as wines from Cyprus and Samos. The girl blushed, the Theatin accepted the invitation, and she followed him, her eyes glued to Candide in confusion and surprise, and clouded with a few tears. No sooner had she set foot in Candide's apartment than she cried out: 'So! Master Candide no longer recognizes Paquette!' At these words, Candide, who had not yet looked at the girl carefully, his thoughts being entirely taken up with Cunégonde, said to her: 'Alas! My poor child, was it you who reduced Doctor Pangloss to the fine state in which I saw him?'

'Alas, sir, it was me.' answered Paquette. 'I see that you know everything. I heard of the frightful disasters that befell the family of my lady Baroness and the fair Cunégonde. I swear to you that my fate has been just as pitiable. When you knew me, I was very innocent. A Franciscan friar, who was my confessor, easily seduced me. The consequences were terrible; I was forced to leave the castle a little while after the Baron had thrown you out with kicks on the backside. If a famous surgeon had not taken pity on me, I should have died. For some time I was this surgeon's mistress, out of gratitude to him. His wife, who was mad with jealousy, beat me mercilessly every day; she was a fury. The surgeon was the ugliest of all men, and I was the most wretched of women, to be continually beaten for a man I did not love. You know, sir, how dangerous it is for an ill-natured woman to be married to a doctor. Incensed at the behaviour of his wife, he one day gave her so effectual a remedy to cure her of a slight cold that she died two hours later in most horrible convulsions. The wife's relatives prosecuted the husband; he took flight, and I was thrown into jail. My innocence would not have saved me if I had not been rather pretty. The judge set me free, on condition that he succeeded the surgeon. But I was soon supplanted by a rival, thrown out quite destitute, and I was obliged to carry on in this abominable trade, which seems so agreeable to you men, while to us women it is the utmost abyss of misery. I have come to exercise the profession in Venice. Ah! Sir, if you could only imagine what it is like to be obliged to caress in the same manner an old merchant, a lawyer, a monk, a gondolier or an abbé; to be exposed to every type of insult and abuse; often to be reduced to borrowing a dress, only to go and have it torn off by a revolting man; to be robbed by one of what you have earned from another; to be subject to the extortions of the officers of justice; and to have nothing to look forward to but a

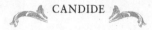

frightful old age, a hospital and a dunghill. You would conclude that I am one of the most unhappy creatures in the world.'

Paquette thus opened her heart to the good Candide, in a closet, in the presence of Martin, who said to his friend: 'You see, I have already won half the wager.'

Friar Giroflée had stayed in the dining-room, and drank a glass or two of wine while he waited for dinner. 'But', said Candide to Paquette, 'you looked so gay and content when I met you; you were singing and you were caressing the Theatin as naturally and tenderly as could be. You seemed to me to be as happy as you now pretend to be the reverse.' – 'Ah! Sir,' answered Paquette, 'that is just another of the miseries of the trade. Yesterday I was robbed and beaten by an officer; yet today I must seem good-humoured to please a friar.'

Candide needed no more convincing; he admitted that Martin was in the right. They sat down to dinner with Paquette and the Theatin; the meal was rather entertaining, and by the end they were talking quite openly. 'Father,' said Candide to the friar, 'you appear to me to enjoy a life that the whole world might envy; you are shining with health, your expression makes plain your happiness; you have a very pretty girl for your recreation, and you seem well satisfied with your position as a Theatin.'

'On my life, sir,' said Friar Giroflée, 'I wish that all the Theatins were at the bottom of the sea. I have been tempted a hundred times to set fire to the monastery and go and become a Turk. At the age of fifteen my parents forced me to put on this detestable habit, so as to leave a greater fortune to a cursed elder brother, God confound him. Jealousy, discord and fury all thrive in the monastery. True, I have preached a few poor sermons that have earned me a little money, of which the prior steals half from me, while the rest goes to pay for girls; but when I return at night to the monastery,

I am ready to dash my head against the walls of the dormitory, and all my fellow friars are in the same state.'

Martin turned towards Candide with his usual coolness. 'Well,' he said, 'have I not won the whole wager?' Candide gave two thousand piastres to Paquette, and one thousand to Friar Giroflée. 'My reply to you', he said, 'is that with this they will be happy.' – 'I don't believe that in the slightest,' said Martin; 'By giving them those piastres you will probably only make them more unhappy still.' – 'Be that as it may,' said Candide, 'but one thing consoles me; I notice that we often meet those whom we expected never to see again. Since I have run into my red sheep and Paquette, it may well be that I will come across Cunégonde.' – 'I hope', said Martin, 'that one day she will make you very happy; but I doubt it very much.' – 'You are a hard man,' said Candide. – 'I have lived,' said Martin.

'But you see those gondoliers,' said Candide, 'do they not sing all the time?' – 'You do not see them at home with their wives and brats,' said Martin. 'The Doge has his troubles, the gondoliers have theirs. It is true that, all things considered, the life of a gondolier is preferable to that of a Doge; but I believe the difference to be so trifling that it is not worth the trouble of examining.'

'People talk', said Candide, 'about the Senator Pococurante,[32] who lives in that fine palazzo on the Brenta, and who is rather welcoming to foreigners. They say that this man has never known any troubles.' – 'I would like to see such a rare species,' said Martin. Candide immediately sent to ask the Lord Pococurante for permission to visit him the following day.

---

32 This is a made-up name meaning Senator 'he who cares little'.

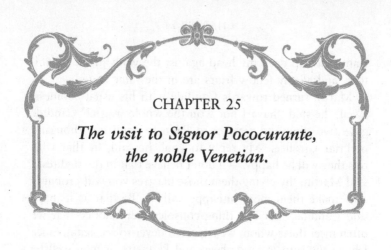

CHAPTER 25

The visit to Signor Pococurante, the noble Venetian.

Candide and Martin went along the Brenta in a gondola and arrived at the palace of the noble Signor Pococurante. The gardens were tastefully designed and adorned with fine marble statues; the palace was beautifully built. The master of the house was a man of sixty, and very rich. He received the two curious travellers with a polite indifference, which disconcerted Candide but rather pleased Martin.

First, two pretty girls, very neatly dressed, served them hot chocolate which was frothed exceedingly well. Candide could not refrain from praising their beauty, grace and skill. 'They are good enough creatures,' said the Senator. 'Sometimes I make them sleep with me, for I am very tired of the ladies of the town, of their coquetries, their jealousies, their quarrels, their moods, their pettiness, their pride, their stupidity, and of the sonnets which one must compose, or have composed, for them; but, on the other hand, I have really begun to tire of these two girls.'

After lunch Candide, walking down a long gallery, was surprised by the beauty of the paintings. He asked which master had painted the first two pictures. 'They are by Raphael,' said the Senator: 'I bought them at a great price, out of vanity, some years ago: they are said to be the finest things in Italy, but they do not please me at all. The colours are too dark, the figures are not sufficiently rounded nor in good relief, and the draperies in no way resemble material. In a word, whatever people say, I do not find them to be a true imitation of nature at all. I only care for a picture when I think I see nature itself; and there are no such pictures. I have a great many pictures, but I do not look at them any more.'

While they were waiting for dinner Pococurante ordered that a *concerto* be performed. Candide found the music delightful. 'This noise', said the Senator, 'may amuse one for half an hour; but if it lasts longer then it becomes tiresome to everybody, though nobody dares admit it. Music today is no more than the art of performing difficult things, and in the long run that which is merely difficult is not entertaining.

'Perhaps I should be fonder of the opera if they had not found the secret of making it into a monster which revolts me. Let who will go to see bad tragedies set to music, where the scenes are contrived solely in order to introduce two or three out-of-place songs to show off an actress's voice. Let who will, or who can, swoon with pleasure at the sight of a eunuch quavering the role of Cæsar or of Cato, and strutting awkwardly on the stage. For my part I have long since renounced those paltry entertainments which constitute the glory of modern Italy, and which are purchased so dearly by sovereigns.' Candide disputed the point a little, but with discretion. Martin was entirely of the Senator's opinion.

They sat down to table, and after an excellent dinner they went into the library. Candide, seeing a magnificently bound volume of Homer, commended the virtuoso on his good taste. 'There', he said 'is a book that was once the delight of the great Pangloss, the best philosopher in Germany.' – 'Well it is not a favourite of mine,' answered Pococurante coldly. 'In the past, others convinced me that I enjoyed reading it, but that continual repetition of battles all so alike; those gods who are always active without doing anything decisive; that

Helen who is the cause of the war and yet scarcely appears in the drama; that Troy so long besieged without being taken; all of it combined to cause in me a near-fatal boredom. I have sometimes asked learned men whether they were not as weary as I of that work. All those who were sincere admitted that the book made them fall asleep, yet it was necessary to have it in their library as a monument of antiquity, or like those rusty coins which are no longer of any value.'

'But surely your Excellency does not think the same of Virgil?' said Candide. – 'I grant', said the Senator, 'that the second, fourth and sixth books of his *Æneid* are excellent, but as for his pious Æneas, his strong Cloanthus, friend Achates, little Ascanius, silly King Latinus, bourgeois Amata and insipid Lavinia, I can think of nothing more flat and disagreeable. I much prefer Tasso, or even the soporific tales of Ariosto.'

'May I presume to ask you, sir,' said Candide, 'whether you do not receive a great deal of pleasure from reading Horace?' – 'There are some maxims in his work', answered Pococurante, 'from which a man of the world can gain profit, and which, as they are compressed into energetic verse, are more easily engraved on the memory. But I care very little for his journey to Brindisi, and his account of a bad dinner, or of his vulgar quarrel with I don't know who – some Pupilus whose words, he says, 'were full of pus', and someone else whose words were 'like vinegar'. It is only with great aversion that I have read his crude verses against old women and witches; nor do I see any merit in telling his friend Mæcenas that, if he will rank him among the lyric poets, his lofty forehead shall touch the stars. Fools admire everything in an author of reputation. I read only to please myself; I like only that which I find useful.' Candide, who had been brought up never to judge anything by himself, was much surprised at what he heard, but Martin found Pococurante's thoughts very reasonable.

'Oh! Here is Cicero,' said Candide. 'As for this great man, I fancy you must never tire of reading him?' – 'I never read him,' replied the Venetian. 'What is it to me whether he pleads for Rabirius or Cluentius? I try enough cases myself. His philosophical works might have suited me better; but, when I realized that he doubted everything, I concluded that I knew as much as he, and that I had no need of a guide to learn ignorance.'

'Ha! Here is an eighty-volume collection of the Academy of Sciences,' cried Martin, 'Perhaps there is something valuable here.' – 'There might be,' said Pococurante, 'if just one of the authors of this rubbish had invented the art of making pins; but in all these volumes there is nothing but empty systems, and not a single useful thing.'

'And what dramatic works I see here!' said Candide, 'In Italian, Spanish and French!' – 'Yes,' replied the Senator, 'there are three thousand, and not three dozen of them are any good. As to those collections of sermons, which all combined are not worth a single page of Seneca, and all those huge volumes of theology, you may well imagine that neither I nor anyone else ever opens them.'

Martin saw some shelves filled with English books. 'I have a notion', said he, 'that a Republican must enjoy most of these books, which are written in such a spirit of freedom.' – 'Yes,' answered Pococurante, 'it is a beautiful thing to write what one thinks; it is the privilege of man. In all Italy, we write only what we do not think; those who inhabit the country of the Cæsars and the Antonines do not even dare to have an idea without the permission of a Dominican monk.[33] I should be pleased with the liberty which inspires the English genius, if passion and party spirit did not corrupt all that is estimable in this precious liberty.'

33 This is a reference to the Dominicans' central role in the Inquisition.

Candide, catching sight of some Milton, asked whether he did not look upon this author as a great man. – 'Who?' said Pococurante, 'That barbarian, who writes a long commentary on the first chapter of Genesis in ten books of harsh verse? That coarse imitator of the Greeks, who disfigures the Creation, and who, while Moses represents the Eternal producing the world by the Word, has the Messiah take a great pair of compasses from some stationery cupboard in heaven to circumscribe His work? How can I have any esteem for a writer who has spoiled Tasso's hell and his devil, who transforms Lucifer sometimes into a toad and sometimes into a pigmy; who makes him repeat the same things a hundred times; who has him disputing points of theology; who, in a serious imitation of Ariosto's comic invention of firearms, has the devils firing cannon in heaven? Neither I nor any man in Italy has been able to enjoy all these melancholy extravagances. The marriage of Sin and Death, and the snakes spawned by Sin, are enough to turn the stomach of any man of refined taste, and his long description of a hospital could interest only a gravedigger. This obscure, bizarre, disgusting poem was despised on its first publication; I treat it now as it was treated in its own country by contemporaries. Besides, I say what I think, and I care very little whether others think as I do.'

Candide was grieved at this speech, for he had a respect for Homer and was fond of Milton. 'Alas!' he said softly to Martin, 'I fear that this man holds our German poets in very great contempt.' – 'There would not be much harm in that,' said Martin. – 'Oh! What a superior man!' Candide continued in hushed tones. 'What a great genius is this Pococurante! Nothing can please him.'

After their survey of the library they went down into the garden, where Candide praised its many beauties. 'I know of nothing in such bad taste,' said the master. 'All you see here is merely trifling; but from tomorrow I will have it planted with a nobler design.'

When the two curious visitors had taken their leave from his Excellency, Candide spoke to Martin: 'So, you will agree that we have just met the happiest of mortals, for he is above everything he owns.' – 'But do you not see', answered Martin, 'that he is disgusted with everything he owns? Plato observed a long while ago that the best stomachs are not those that reject all sorts of food.' – 'But is there not pleasure to be found', said Candide, 'in criticizing everything, in pointing out faults where others see nothing but beauty?' – 'Do you mean', replied Martin, 'that there is pleasure in having no pleasure?' – 'Oh, have it your way,' said Candide. 'So I will be the only happy man in the world, when I see dear Cunégonde again.' – 'It is always well to hope,' said Martin.

However, the days and the weeks passed. Cacambo did not come, and Candide was so overwhelmed with grief that he did not even reflect that Paquette and Friar Giroflée had not returned to thank him.

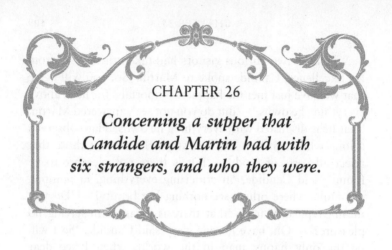

CHAPTER 26

Concerning a supper that Candide and Martin had with six strangers, and who they were.

One evening when Candide, followed by Martin, was about to sit down to supper with some foreigners staying at the same inn, a man whose complexion was black as soot approached him from behind and taking him by the arm, said: 'Get ready to leave with us; do not fail.' Upon this he turned round and saw – Cacambo! Nothing but the sight of Cunégonde could have astonished and delighted him more. He was on the point of going mad with joy. He embraced his dear friend. 'Cunégonde is here, without doubt; where is she? Take me to her so that I may die of joy in her company.' – 'Cunégonde is not here,' said Cacambo, 'she is in Constantinople.' – 'Oh, heavens! In Constantinople! But were she in China I would fly to her; let's go!' – 'We will leave after supper,' replied Cacambo. 'I can tell you nothing more; I am a slave, my master awaits me, I must serve him at table. Don't say a word; eat, and then get ready.'

Candide, torn between joy and grief, delighted at seeing his faithful agent again, astonished at finding him a slave, filled with the fresh hope of recovering his mistress, his heart palpitating, his faculties overwhelmed, sat down to table with Martin, who observed all these scenes quite calmly, and with six foreigners who had come to enjoy the Carnival in Venice.

Cacambo waited at table on one of these strangers. Towards the end of the entertainment he drew near his master and spoke in his ear: 'Sire, your Majesty may start when he pleases, the vessel is ready.' On saying these words he went out. The company, astounded, looked at one another without speaking a word, when another domestic approached his master and said to him: 'Sire, your Majesty's chaise is at Padua, and the boat is ready.' The master gave a nod and the servant went away. The company all stared at one another again, in even greater surprise. A third valet came up to a third stranger, saying: 'Sire, believe me, your Majesty ought not to stay here any longer. I am going to get everything ready,' and immediately he disappeared.

Candide and Martin no longer doubted that this must be some Carnival masquerade. Then a fourth domestic said to a fourth master: 'Your Majesty may depart whenever he pleases,' and went away like the rest. The fifth valet said the same thing to the fifth master. But the sixth valet spoke differently to the sixth stranger, who sat near Candide. He said to him: 'Well, Sire, they will no longer give credit to your Majesty nor to me, and we could both be put in jail this very night; I must take care of my own affairs. Adieu.'

When all the servants had gone, the six strangers, with Candide and Martin, remained in a profound silence. At last Candide broke it. 'Gentlemen,' he said, 'this is a very strange joke indeed, how can you all be kings?[34] As for me, I own that neither Martin nor I is a king.'

34 The six rulers mentioned are Achmet III of Turkey, who ruled from 1703 to 1730 when he was dethroned; Ivan VI of Russia (b. 1740, d. 1764) who was dethroned in 1741 while he was still a baby; Charles Edward Stuart (b. 1720, d. 1788), known as the Young Pretender; Augustus III (b. 1696, d. 1763), King of Poland; Stanislaus I (b. 1682, d. 1766), King of Poland; and Theodore (b. 1690, d. 1755), who was several times proclaimed King of Corsica. Although it is impossible for these six kings ever to have met, five of them could have been made to do so without any anachronism.

Cacambo's master then gravely answered in Italian: 'I am not joking at all. My name is Achmet III. I was Grand Sultan for many years. I dethroned my brother; my nephew dethroned me, my viziers had their throats cut; I am living out my days in the old seraglio. My nephew, the great Sultan Mahmoud, permits me to travel sometimes for my health, and I have come to spend the Carnival in Venice.'

A young man who sat next to Achmet then spoke as follows: 'My name is Ivan. I was once Emperor of all the Russias, but I was dethroned in my cradle. My parents were locked up and I was brought up in prison; yet I am sometimes allowed to travel, accompanied by my guards, and I have come to spend the Carnival in Venice.'

The third said: 'I am Charles Edward, King of England; my father has resigned all his rights over the kingdom to me. I have fought hard to defend them. Eight hundred of my supporters have had their hearts torn out and their cheeks slapped with them. I have been imprisoned. I am going to Rome to pay a visit to the King, my father, who was dethroned like myself and my grandfather, and I have come to spend the Carnival in Venice.'

The fourth then spoke up: 'I am the King of the Poles; the fortunes of war have stripped me of my hereditary dominions. My father suffered the same setbacks. I resign myself to Providence in the same manner as Sultan Achmet, the Emperor Ivan and King Charles Edward, may God long preserve them; and I have come to spend the Carnival in Venice.'

The fifth said: 'I am also King of the Poles. I have lost my kingdom twice; but Providence has given me another country, where I have done more good than all the Sarmatian kings were ever capable of doing on the banks of the Vistula. I likewise resign myself to Providence, and have come to spend the Carnival in Venice.'

It was now the sixth monarch's turn to speak: 'Gentlemen,' he said, 'I am not so great a prince as any of you, but I have

been a king like everyone else. My name is Theodore, I was elected King of Corsica; I had the title of Majesty, and now I am scarcely treated as a gentleman. I have coined money, and now I do not have a penny. I have had two secretaries of state, and now I scarcely have a valet; I have sat on a throne, and I have languished on straw in a common jail in London. I am afraid that I shall meet with the same treatment here, though, like your majesties, I have come to spend the Carnival in Venice.'

The other five kings listened to this speech with a most noble compassion. Each of them gave twenty sequins to King Theodore to buy clothes and linen; and Candide made him a present of a diamond worth two thousand sequins. 'Who can this commoner be?' the five kings asked one another. 'Who is able to give a hundred times more than any of us, and who moreover has actually given it?'

Just as they were leaving the table, there arrived at the same hotel four serene highnesses who had also been stripped of their territories by the fortunes of war, and had come to spend the Carnival in Venice. But Candide paid no regard to these newcomers. He thought only of his voyage to Constantinople, in search of his beloved Cunégonde.

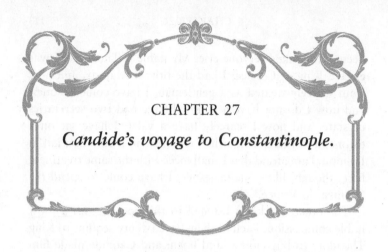

CHAPTER 27

Candide's voyage to Constantinople.

The faithful Cacambo had already prevailed upon the Turkish skipper who was conducting Sultan Achmet to Constantinople to receive Candide and Martin on his ship. They both set off after prostrating themselves before his miserable Highness. On the way, Candide said to Martin, 'There, you see, we supped with six dethroned kings, and of those six there was one to whom I gave alms. Perhaps there are many other princes yet more unfortunate. For my part, I have only lost a hundred sheep; and now I am flying to Cunégonde's embrace. My dear Martin, yet again Pangloss was right: everything is well.'

'I hope so,' answered Martin. – 'But', said Candide, 'what a very strange situation that was in Venice. Who ever saw, or heard of, six dethroned kings supping together in a tavern?' – 'It is no more extraordinary', said Martin, 'than most of the things that have happened to us. It is a very common thing for kings to be dethroned; and as for the honour we had of supping in their company, it is a trifle not worth our attention.'

No sooner had Candide boarded the vessel than he threw his arms about the neck of his old valet and friend Cacambo. 'So!' he said, 'What news of Cunégonde? Is she still a prodigious beauty? Does she love me still? How is she? You have no doubt bought her a palace in Constantinople?'

'My dear master,' answered Cacambo, 'Cunégonde washes dishes on the banks of the Propontis, in the service of a prince who has very few dishes. She is a slave in the family of an old ruler named Ragotsky, to whom the Grand Turk allows three crowns a day in his exile. But what is much worse still is that she has lost her beauty and become horribly ugly.' – 'Well, handsome or ugly,' replied Candide, 'I am a man of honour, and it is my duty to love her always. But how came she to be reduced to so abject a state with the five or six million that you took to her?' – 'Well,' said Cacambo, 'was I not to give two million to Senor Don Fernando d'Ibaraa, y Figueora, y Mascarenes, y Lampourdos, y Souza, Governor of Buenos Aires, for the permission to take back Miss Cunégonde? And did a pirate not gallantly rob us of all the rest? And what did this pirate do, but take us to Cape Matapan, to Milo, to Nicaria, to Samos, to Petra, to the Dardanelles, to Marmora and to Scutari? Cunégonde and the old woman now serve the prince I just mentioned, and I am slave to the dethroned Sultan.' – 'What a series of appalling calamities!' cried Candide. 'But after all, I still have some diamonds left; I can easily pay Cunégonde's ransom. But it is a real pity that she is grown so ugly.'

Then, turning to Martin: 'Who do you think', he asked, 'is most to be pitied – the Sultan Achmet, the Emperor Ivan, King Charles Edward or myself?' – 'I have no idea,' answered Martin. 'I would have to be able to see into your hearts to be able to tell.' – 'Ah!' said Candide, 'If Pangloss were here, he would know, and he would tell us.' – 'I do not know', said Martin, 'with what sort of scales your Pangloss would have been able weigh the misfortunes of mankind and quantify their sorrows. All that I can presume to say is that there are millions of people on this earth who have a hundred times more to complain of than King Charles Edward, the Emperor Ivan, or the Sultan Achmet.' – 'That may well be so,' said Candide.

In a few days they reached the Bosphorus, and Candide began by paying a very high ransom for Cacambo. Then, with no further ado, he and his companions leapt on board a galley to head for the shores of the Propontis and search for his Cunégonde, however ugly she might be.

Among the galley crew were two slaves who rowed very badly, whose bare shoulders the Levantine captain now and then thrashed with a stick. Candide, from a natural impulse, looked at these two slaves more attentively than at the other oarsmen, and approached them with pity. Their features, though greatly disfigured, seemed to him to bear a slight resemblance to those of Pangloss and the unhappy Jesuit and Westphalian Baron, brother to Miss Cunégonde. This thought moved and saddened him. He looked at them still more attentively. 'Indeed,' he said to Cacambo, 'if I had not seen Master Pangloss hanged, and if I had not had the misfortune to kill the Baron, I should think it was they who were rowing.'

At the names of the Baron and of Pangloss, the two galley slaves let out a loud cry, stopped rowing and let drop their oars. The Levantine captain ran up to them and stepped up his thrashing. 'Stop! Stop, sir!' cried Candide. 'I will give you as much money as you want.' – 'What! It is Candide!' said one of the slaves. – 'What! It is Candide!' said the other. – 'Is this a dream?' cried Candide, 'Am I awake? Am I on board this galley? Is this the Baron whom I killed? Is this Master Pangloss whom I saw hanged?'

'It is we! It is we!' they replied. – 'Well! Is this the great philosopher?' said Martin.

'Ah! Captain,' said Candide, 'how much ransom do you want for Monsieur de Thunder-ten-Tronckh, one of the first barons of the Empire, and for Monsieur Pangloss, the profoundest metaphysician in all of Germany?' – 'Dog of a Christian,' answered the Levantine captain, 'since these two dogs of Christian slaves are barons and metaphysicians, which I've no doubt are high honours in their country, you shall

give me fifty thousand sequins.' – 'You shall have them, sir.
Take me straight back to Constantinople, and you shall receive
the money directly. But no, first take me to Miss Cunégonde.'
But the Levantine captain had already tacked about on
Candide's first offer, and made the crew row quicker than a
bird cleaves the air.

Candide embraced the Baron and Pangloss a hundred
times. 'And how come, my dear Baron, that I did not kill
you? And my dear Pangloss, how come you are alive after
being hanged? And why are you both in a Turkish galley?'

'Is it really true that my dear sister is in this country?' said
the Baron. – 'Yes,' replied Cacambo. – 'So I see my dear
Candide once again,' cried Pangloss. Candide presented Martin
and Cacambo to them; they all embraced one another, and all
spoke at once. The galley flew; they were already in the port.
Candide sent for a Jew, to whom he sold for fifty thousand
sequins a diamond worth a hundred thousand, and who swore
by Abraham that he could give him no more. He immediately
paid the ransom for the Baron and Pangloss. The latter threw
himself at the feet of his liberator and bathed them with his
tears; the former thanked him with a nod, and promised to
pay the money back at the first opportunity. – 'But is it really
possible that my sister can be in Turkey?' he said. – 'Nothing
is more possible,' said Cacambo, 'since she scours the dishes
in the service of a Transylvanian prince.' Two more Jews were
sent for; Candide sold them some more diamonds, and then
they all set out together in another galley to free Cunégonde
from slavery.

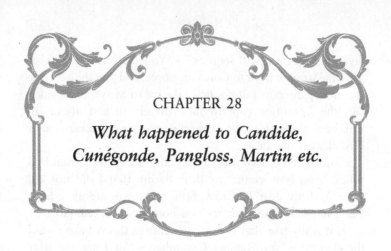

'Once again, please forgive me,' said Candide to the Baron, 'forgive me, Reverend Father, for running you through the body with my sword.'

'Say no more about it,' answered the Baron. 'I was a little too hasty, I admit. But since you wish to know by what twist of fate I came to be a galley slave, here is my story: after I had been cured by the college apothecary of the wound you gave me, I was attacked and abducted by a party of Spanish troops, who threw me into prison at Buenos Aires at the very time my sister was leaving the city. I asked leave to return to Rome with the General of my Order; then I was appointed chaplain to the French Ambassador in Constantinople. I had only been in this employment a week or so, when one evening I met with a young *icoglan*,[35] who was a very handsome fellow. The weather was hot and the young man wanted to bathe, so I too took the opportunity to bathe. I did not know that it was a capital offence for a Christian to be found naked with a young Muslim. A cadi[36] ordered me a hundred strokes on the soles of the feet, and condemned me to the galleys. I do not think there has ever been a greater act of injustice. But I should very

35 A boy in the Sultan's seraglio.
36 A Muslim judge.

much like to know how my sister came to be kitchen-maid to a Transylvanian prince who has taken shelter among the Turks.'

'But you, my dear Pangloss,' said Candide, 'how can it be that I behold you again?'

'It is true,' said Pangloss, 'that you saw me hanged. Of course I should have been burned alive, but you may remember it was pouring with rain when they were going to roast me; the storm was so violent that they despaired of lighting the fire, so I was hanged because that was the best they could do. A surgeon purchased my corpse, took me home, and dissected me. He began with making a crucial incision on me from the navel to the collarbone. But one could not have been hanged more badly than I had been. The executioner of the Holy Inquisition was a sub-deacon, and knew how to burn people marvellously well, but he was not accustomed to hanging: the rope was wet through and did not slip properly, and besides it was knotted – in short, I was still breathing. The crucial incision made me let out such a frightful scream that my surgeon fell over backwards, and thinking that he had been dissecting the devil he ran away in a mortal terror, falling down the staircase in his flight. His wife, hearing the noise, ran in from the next room. She saw me stretched out on the table with my crucial incision; she was seized with yet greater fear than her husband, fled, and tumbled over him. When they had recovered themselves a little, I heard the surgeon's wife say to her husband: 'My dear, how could you take it into your head to dissect a heretic? Don't you know that such people always have the devil in their bodies? I will go and fetch a priest this minute to exorcise him.' At this proposal I shuddered, and mustering up what little strength remained to me I cried out, 'Have mercy on me!' Finally the Portuguese barber[37] plucked up his spirits and sewed me up; his wife even nursed me, and after fifteen days I was back on my feet.

---

37 Until the eighteenth century, barbers used routinely to carry out surgery; they were known as barber-surgeons.

The barber found me a position as footman to a Knight of Malta who was going to Venice, but finding that my master had no money to pay my wages, I entered the service of a Venetian merchant, and went to Constantinople with him.

'One day I took it into my head to step inside a mosque, where I saw an old Imam and a very pretty young devotee who was saying her paternosters. Her bosom was uncovered, and between her breasts she had a beautiful bouquet of tulips, roses, anemones, buttercups, hyacinths and primulas. She dropped her bouquet; I picked it up, and put it back in its place with a most respectful zeal. I took so long arranging it that the Imam began to get angry, and seeing that I was a Christian he called out for help. They dragged me before the cadi, who ordered me a hundred lashes on the soles of the feet and sent me to the galleys. I was chained in the very same galley and on the same bench as Monsieur the Baron. On board this galley there were four young men from Marseilles, five Neapolitan priests and two monks from Corfu, who told us that such things happen all the time. The Baron maintained that he had suffered greater injustice than I, and I insisted that it was far more innocent to pick up a bouquet and put it back on a woman's bosom than to be found stark naked with an *icoglan*. We were arguing continually, and receiving twenty lashes a day, when the concatenation of universal events brought you to our galley and you ransomed us.'

'And so, my dear Pangloss,' Candide asked him, 'when you had been hanged, dissected, thrashed, and rowed in the galley, did you ever stop believing that everything happens for the best?'

'I am still of my first opinion,' answered Pangloss, 'for I am a philosopher and it wouldn't be right to retract, since Leibniz could never be wrong and pre-established harmony is moreover the finest thing in the world, as are the *plenum* and *materia subtilis*.'[38]

38　These Cartesian terms refer to Leibniz's belief in a universe 'full' of matter, denying the possibility of void space.

CHAPTER 29

*How Candide found Cunégonde
and the old woman again.*

While Candide, the Baron, Pangloss, Martin and Cacambo were relating their adventures, were reasoning on the contingent or non-contingent events of the universe, disputing on effects and causes, on moral and physical evil, on liberty and necessity, and on the consolations that even a slave on a Turkish galley may feel, they arrived at the house of the Transylvanian prince on the banks of the Propontis. The first thing they saw was Cunégonde and the old woman hanging towels out to dry.

The Baron paled at this sight. The tender lover Candide, seeing his beautiful Cunégonde sunburned, with blood-shot eyes, withered breasts, wrinkled cheeks and rough, red arms, recoiled three paces in horror, and then advanced out of good manners. She embraced Candide and her brother; they embraced the old woman, and Candide ransomed them both.

There was a small farm in the neighbourhood; the old woman proposed that Candide manage with that until the whole company should enjoy better fortune. Cunégonde did not know she had grown ugly since no one had told her, and she reminded Candide of his promises in such a categorical manner that he did not dare refuse her. So he told the Baron that he intended to marry his sister. 'I will not suffer', said the Baron, 'such a base fortune for her, and such insolence from you. I will never be reproached for such a scandal; my sister's children would never be able to enter the Chapters[39] of Germany. No; my sister shall only marry a baron of the Empire.' Cunégonde flung herself at his feet and bathed them in tears; still he was inflexible. 'You foolish man,' said Candide; 'I have freed you from the galleys, I have paid your ransom and your sister's; she was a kitchen-maid, and she is ugly, I am so generous as to marry her, and yet you insist on opposing the match? I would kill you again, were I to give in to my anger.' – 'Kill me again, then,' said the Baron, 'but you will not marry my sister so long as I live.'

---

39 Assemblies of the clergy and nobility.

CHAPTER 30

Conclusion.

At the bottom of his heart Candide had no wish to marry Cunégonde. But the extreme impertinence of the Baron determined him to carry it through, and Cunégonde pressed him so urgently that he couldn't go back on his promise. He consulted Pangloss, Martin and the faithful Cacambo. Pangloss drew up an excellent memorandum, in which he proved that the Baron had no rights over his sister, and that she could, in accordance with all the laws of the Empire, marry Candide with her left hand.[40] Martin was for throwing the Baron into the sea. Cacambo decided that they should return him to the Levantine captain to be put back in the galley, after which they would send him back to the General Father of the Order at Rome by the first ship. This advice was well received, and the old woman approved it. They said not a word to the Baron's sister; the plan was executed for a small sum, and they had the double pleasure of netting a Jesuit and punishing the pride of a German baron.

It is natural to imagine that after so many disasters Candide, married to his mistress, living with the philosopher Pangloss, the philosopher Martin, the prudent Cacambo and

40 A morganatic marriage, between a couple of unequal social rank, in which no property or titles are conferred on the spouse.

the old woman, and what's more with so many diamonds from the country of the ancient Incas, might have led a very happy life. But he was so comprehensively fleeced by the Jews that in the end he had nothing left except his small farm; his wife became uglier every day, more bitter and intolerable; the old woman was an invalid and even more fretful than Cunégonde. Cacambo, who worked in the garden and took vegetables for sale to Constantinople, was over-worked, and cursed his destiny. Pangloss was in despair at not shining in some German university. As for Martin, he was firmly persuaded that he would be just as badly off elsewhere, so he bore things patiently. Candide, Martin and Pangloss sometimes argued about morals and metaphysics. From the windows of the farmhouse they often saw boats pass by full of effendis, pashas and cadis who were being exiled to Lemnos, Mitylene or Erzerum. They saw other cadis, pashas, and effendis coming to take the place of the exiles, who were later exiled in their turn. They saw well-impaled heads being taken for display at the Sublime Porte.[41] These spectacles increased the number of their discussions. When they did not argue, time hung so heavily on their hands that one day the old woman ventured to say to them: 'I want to know which is worse, to be raped a hundred times by negro pirates, to have a buttock cut off, to run the gauntlet of the Bulgar soldiers, to be whipped and hanged at an *auto-da-fé*, to be dissected, to row in the galleys – in short, to go through all the miseries we have undergone – or to stay here and have nothing to do?' – 'It is a great question,' said Candide.

This speech gave rise to new reflections, and Martin in particular concluded that man was born to live either in a state of convulsive anxiety or of lethargic boredom. Candide did not agree, but he didn't confirm why. Pangloss admitted that he had always suffered horribly, but as he had once

41 The gate of the Sultan's palace.

asserted that everything was going marvellously, he continued to assert it, though he no longer believed it.

Then something happened that confirmed Martin in his detestable principles, made Candide more hesitant than ever, and embarrassed Pangloss: one day they witnessed Paquette and Friar Giroflée arrive at their farm in the most extreme poverty. They had soon squandered their three thousand piastres, left each other, been reconciled, quarrelled again, been thrown into jail, escaped, and finally Friar Giroflée had become a Turk. Paquette continued to ply her trade wherever she went, but no longer made any money from it. 'I predicted only too well', said Martin to Candide, 'that your gifts would soon be squandered, and only serve to make them more miserable. You have rolled in millions of piastres, you and Cacambo, and yet you are no happier than Friar Giroflée and Paquette.' – 'Aha!' said Pangloss to Paquette, 'So heaven has brought you amongst us again, my poor child! Do you know that you cost me the tip of my nose, an eye and an ear? And look at you! What a world this is!' And this new turn of events set them to philosophizing more than ever.

In the neighbourhood there lived a very famous Dervish who was judged to be the best philosopher in all Turkey, and they went to consult him. Pangloss was the speaker. 'Master,' he said, 'we have come to ask you to tell why so strange an animal as man was created.'

'Why are you interfering?' said the Dervish; 'is it any of your business?' – 'But, Reverend Father,' said Candide, 'there is horrible evil in this world.' – 'What does it matter', said the Dervish, 'whether there is evil or good? When his Highness sends a ship to Egypt, does he trouble his head whether the mice on board are comfortable or not?' – 'So what should we do?' asked Pangloss. – 'Keep quiet,' answered the Dervish. – 'I was rather hoping', said Pangloss, 'that we would have a little discussion about effects and causes, about the best of

possible worlds, the origin of evil, the nature of the soul, and the pre-established harmony.' At these words, the Dervish shut the door in their faces.

During this conversation, the news was spread that two viziers and a mufti[42] had been strangled in Constantinople, and that several of their friends had been impaled. This catastrophe caused an uproar for several hours. Pangloss, Candide and Martin, on their way back to the little farm, saw an honourable old man at his door taking some fresh air under an orange bower. Pangloss, who was as inquisitive as he was argumentative, asked the old man the name of the strangled mufti. 'I have no idea,' answered the worthy man, 'and I have never known the name of any mufti, nor of any vizier. I am entirely ignorant of the events you mention. I presume in general that those who meddle with the affairs of state sometimes die miserably, and that they deserve it, but I never trouble my head about what is going on in Constantinople; I content myself with sending fruit there to sell from the garden I cultivate.'

Having spoken these words, he invited the strangers into his house. His two sons and two daughters presented them with several sorts of sorbet which they made themselves, with *kaimak* spiced with the candied citron peel, with oranges, lemons, pineapples, pistachio nuts and some mocha coffee unadulterated with bad coffee from Batavia or the American islands. After which the two daughters of this honest Muslim perfumed the beards of Candide, Pangloss and Martin.

'You must have a vast and magnificent estate,' said Candide to the Turk. 'I have only twenty acres,' replied the Turk; 'I cultivate them along with my children; the work preserves us from three great evils – weariness, vice and want.'

Candide, on his way home, reflected deeply on the old man's words. 'This honest Turk', he said to Pangloss and

---

42 Two ministers and a religious dignitary.

Martin, 'seems to have made for himself an existence far preferable to that of the six kings with whom we had the honour of dining.'

'Grandeur', said Pangloss, 'is extremely dangerous, according to the testimony of all the philosophers. Take for example Eglon, King of the Moabites, who was assassinated by Ehud; Absalom, hung by his hair and pierced with three darts; King Nadab, son of Jeroboam, killed by Baasa; King Elah by Zimri; Ahaziah by Jehu; Athaliah by Jehoiada; and Kings Jehoiakim, Jeconiah and Zedekiah, who were enslaved. You know how perished Croesus, Astyages, Darius, Dionysius of Syracuse, Pyrrhus, Perseus, Hannibal, Jugurtha, Ariovistus, Cæsar, Pompey, Nero, Otho, Vitellius, Domitian, Richard II of England, Edward II, Henry VI, Richard III, Mary Stuart, Charles I, the three Henrys of France and the Emperor Henry IV! You know...' – 'I also know', said Candide, 'that we should cultivate our garden.' – 'You are right,' said Pangloss, 'for when man was first placed in the Garden of Eden, he was put there *ut operaretur eum*, that he might cultivate it; which shows that man was not born to be idle.' – 'Let us get to work,' said Martin, 'without philosophizing; it is the only way to render life tolerable.'

The whole little society entered into this laudable plan, each according to their different abilities. Their little plot of land produced plentiful crops. Cunégonde was, it must be said, very ugly, but she became an excellent pastry cook; Paquette worked at embroidery; the old woman took care of the linen. They were all, Friar Giroflée included, of some service or other; for he made a good joiner, and even became a decent man.

Pangloss sometimes said to Candide: 'There is a concatenation of events in this best of all possible worlds: for after all, if you had not been kicked out of a magnificent castle for love of Miss Cunégonde, if you had not been tried before

the Inquisition, if you had not crossed America on foot, if you had not given the Baron a good running-through with your sword, if you had not lost all your sheep from the fine country of El Dorado, you would not be here eating candied citron and pistachio nuts.' – 'Well said,' replied Candide, 'but let us cultivate our garden.'